Emerald

Garry Richardson

For Permission requests, write to:
YBR Publishing, LLC
PO Box 4904
Beaufort SC 29903-4904
contact@ybrpub.com
843-900-0859

GARRY RICHARDSON

ISBN-13: 979-8-9852082-0-7

Cover art by Sarah Stowe
The Stowe Gallery of Fine Arts
www.stowe.gallery

YBR PUBLISHING, LLC

Jack Gannon – Co-Owner, Production Manager
Cyndi Williams-Barnier – Co-Owner, Production Editor
Bill Barnier – Co-Owner, Senior Editor
Loreen Ridge-Husum – Art Director
Michelle Owens – Marketing Agent

"I dropped a tear in the ocean, and whenever they find it, I'll stop loving you…"

~Natalie Campbell

ACKNOWLEDGEMENTS

First of all, I'd like to thank God for blessing me with a small amount of talent, a passion for reading and the life I've lived so far.

To my wife, Katie, and my children, Forrest and Emma, I'd like to say thanks for supporting me while I spent hours writing on a laptop. I hope this serves as a lesson to follow your dreams no matter how crazy they may seem.

I'd also like to thank my mom for giving me a love for reading at an early age, and my dad for the work ethic it would take to work full time and take on a project like this.

To Bill Barnier, the Editor Supreme: you deserve most of the credit for how this came out. Without your help, knowledge, friendship and perseverance (not to mention patience), this would never have become reality. To YBR Publishing: thank you for taking a chance on an unknown writer with a lot of stories rattling around in his head but little talent for actually writing them.

Thank you to Sarah Stowe for the awesome cover art, I couldn't imagine a better cover.

To everyone who has read this, from the early versions to what's before you: thank you for the encouragement, kind words, and the time it took for you to read it.

Finally, to the person reading this book: thank you for the investment of your time, I pray by the end it pays off!

This book is dedicated to my wife Katie. Without you, I would have never have known what love is.

Foreword

Emerald began on my way to and from work. With a thirty-minute drive each way, I formed the first few chapters without ever writing anything down. But I began to have feelings for the characters and knew I needed to write to keep everything straight and to get it out of my head. I never thought anyone would be interested in it or would ever read it. I offered it to a friend to read, never expecting it would go anywhere. Writing *Emerald* gave me immense satisfaction and a chance to grow as an author. I hope you enjoy the journey you're about to take with Sam, Macy and the Old Man; it was fun for me to live in their world for a while. Maybe it will be for you as well.

~Garry Richardson

Chapter 1

The sailboat sliced through the gentle swells like a sharp knife. Behind the wheel, the old man stood silent, watchful, unconcerned that his craft looked like it would tip over at any moment. Hours earlier he found the sweet spot where wind and sea were in perfect harmony with the sleek hull and full sail, making the miles pass effortlessly.

Tanned from decades under the nautical sun, the old man was dressed in a sun-bleached tan fishing shirt and faded shorts that began life dark green. A well-worn pair of deck shoes and a wide brimmed floppy hat provided cover for his head and feet. Behind a pair of Wayfarer sunglasses his chocolate brown eyes shifted between the sails and sea. Long years of sailing made his vigilance a habit, where solace and comfort replaced anxiety.

Cotton ball clouds dotted the cobalt sky, promising good weather for the day. He grunted at his own hubris in predicting the ever-changing weather of the Atlantic Ocean. More than once it had proven the old man wrong. Off the port side of his fifty-foot sailboat, toward the mainland, he could see the dark gray tops of the mountains, a brown and green smear on the horizon, miles inland. He estimated his speed at 23 knots, not bad for a boat nearly as old as he. Seeing nothing on the water that required his attention, he rechecked his heading on the chart clipped next to him. He was sailing north for the first time in many years, to a place from deep in his past. He wondered if his ninety-five-year old body could take such a long and arduous journey. But she summoned him and there was never a question he would not go to her. With all he'd lived through, a trip of 5500 miles was just another test of his endurance. The thought made him smile, he would endure this like a great many other things, though the adversary on this trip was time, not distance. He knew his end time was coming. He watched death take too many in his time and recalled the look in the eyes of old men whose hourglass was down to a few final grains of sand. The thought of her and sand, mingled with the sails and the sea, reminded him of the first time he'd seen her. He marveled at how fast time had passed. Checking the sails again, he let his mind drift back to 1989, when he was eighteen.

Sam and his best friend, Alex, decided to do something different on one of their rare days off. The pair drove across the South Carolina state line into Georgia, heading for the beaches of Tybee Island where they would stake out an area among the tourists and watch the young tanned beauties parade across the sand or splashing in the surf. Alex stepped into the water to cool off and get closer to a girl he was interested in, while Sam decided to take a walk down the beach. He was a half mile away when he spotted a group of people gathered around a collection of small sailboats. They were small two-man ketches, surrounded by their crews making last-minute checks on their sleek sailing crafts. Curious as to what was going on, Sam walked over and listened to a man who was shouting to be heard over the waves, gulls, and wind.

"The circuit is out and back twice. Keep it safe and clean; if you're tagged for a penalty then make your penalty loop and continue on. Good luck." The teams broke up and headed for their boats to get them in the water. Sam walked up to the man who had shouted out the rules.

"What's going on?"

The man glanced at him, and then went back to watching the crews raising their sails, school emblems displayed proudly on the canvas.

"It's a regatta. There are colleges from across the East Coast competing for the Tybee Cup."

Intrigued, Sam found a place where he could watch. The course was made up of two buoys, one red and one green, placed several hundred yards apart. The man on the beach watched the boats gather and turn toward the red buoy, then raised an air horn and blew a long blast to signal the start. The buoys were parallel to the shore and the two-man teams would be starting on the downwind leg. The small crowd watching the regatta let out cheers when the first boats reached the buoys. After the turn, a couple of boats had to make an extra 360-degree turn, around the green buoy, to serve their penalty for bumping into other competitors. With their turns complete, they hurried to chase down the teams ahead of them. Those not serving a penalty stretched their lead on the upwind leg, the wind blowing at them head on. To combat the headwind, the sailboats began to tack away from the beach, racing for deeper water and room to maneuver. Two boats slowly separated from the pack, creating a battle for the lead. The two top teams were from Duke University and the University of Miami. Sam found himself pulling for the Duke team over the team from Florida. At the second turn, the Miami team pulled out to a slight lead by cutting in close to the buoy, but the Duke team caught them on the downwind leg entering the last turn. The two boats were side by side when they reached the red buoy, but once again, the Miami team eased into the lead through the turn. Both teams tacked away from the shore, a few yards separating their battle for wind and the lead. The Miami team turned hard, forcing the Duke sailors to dodge them or risk a penalty. Coming to the finish line, the Duke team couldn't close the gap. The competitors turned toward the shore and landed their boats on the beach.

Sam walked over to the defeated Duke team while everyone else crowded around the winners. He came up behind a crew member wearing a Blue Devils ball cap, tan shorts and a bright yellow life vest over a white shirt. "Good race."

The crewman turned, catching him by surprise. Under the cap was a pair of sparkling green eyes on the face of a beautiful girl. She looked him over and turned back to finish her work.

"Thanks, we should have won that one."

Her partner grunted.

"Will you let it go already?"

"If you had just listened to me instead of being an ass, we would have won the cup, Dean."

"Remember, I'm the captain of this team and your ride back to Raleigh. Unless you want to walk back to school, shut up," He barked.

Sam stepped between them. "You need to change your tone, bud. You don't talk to a lady that way."

"I don't remember asking your opinion," Dean said, poking his chest out in challenge.

Sam stepped forward to accept his challenge and felt a hand grab his arm.

"Please, don't."

Sam paused long enough to look at her. "You don't have to take any crap off him. He needs a lesson in manners."

The race coordinator appeared and took in the scene at a glance. "Is there a problem here?"

"No, sir, he was just asking about the ketch and how it works," the girl answered while the two boys stared at each other, each waiting on the other to make a move.

The man looked at Sam, and then turned to Dean. "I need all the team captains to sign their time sheets. They're at the coordinator's table."

Dean gave Sam another challenging look before stalking off toward the tent to sign the paperwork. The girl shook her head slowly.

"Were you really going to fight him over me? He's a senior and I'm just a sophomore."

"For you, I'd take on the whole senior class."

She rolled her eyes, but smiled in spite of herself. "Well, Superman, thanks for coming to the rescue, but Dean's harmless."

"I was always more of a Batman fan, but you're welcome. Are you busy later? I could show you the Bat Cave. Sam Richards," he said, holding out his hand. She reached out, putting her hand in his.

"Macy McCoy, and as much as I would like to, I have plans." Sam looked disappointed with her reply.

"Okay, but remember, if you need a superhero, just signal," he said, turning to leave. "Wait, I have an award dinner to attend and I could use a date. You interested?"

Sam's smile turned into a grin. "Just tell me when and where."

She walked to the coordinator's table, grabbed a pen, and then wrote the address and time on the back of his hand.

"The dress code is casual, but bring a change of clothes. The real party begins after." She pecked him on the cheek and returned to the sailboat to finish breaking it down. Sam watched her walk away and laughed at his luck. He went back in search of Alex to tell him it was time to go home.

Four hours later, dressed in dark blue pants and a blue-and-white striped shirt, Sam arrived at the door of a yellow two-story house. A sign hanging on the stairs leading to the front door read, "The Shell House". A tanned guy in a Florida State tee shirt opened the door when he knocked.

"What's up, dude?" the guy asked, looking at Sam oddly.

"I'm looking for the girl from the Duke sailing team," Sam told him.

"Come on in, man, she's upstairs somewhere, I think," the guy said, turning his attention to a girl walking past and forgetting Sam.

Sam reached the foot of the stairs and was starting his climb when Macy came out of one of the rooms. She was dressed in a short white sundress, with her black hair pulled up into a ponytail. She didn't see him at first and was three steps down when she noticed.

"Oh," she said as she looked him up and down, and then raised her eyebrow. "You clean up nice."

"So do you." He held out his hand, which she accepted, descending to the step above him. He stared into her eyes while he held her hand, until she looked away.

"We don't want to be late," she told him.

He led her outside to his old Chevy truck. He opened her door, helping her inside.

"Sorry, the Bat-mobile had a flat tire," he joked, closing her door.

"Maybe we can take it next time," she replied while he climbed behind the wheel.

She gave him directions to where the ceremony was taking place. The ball room was crowded and with all of the conversations going on at the same time, it was too loud to concentrate. There was a small buffet of finger foods and punch. Macy introduced different members of the sailing teams while they walked through the room to find their seats.

"Is your partner going to be here tonight?" Sam asked, seeing the place cards on the table.

Macy shook her head. "He said he wouldn't be attending unless we won."

Sam laughed as he picked up his glass, "Well, then, here's to second place and great company." Macy laughed, picking up her glass before tapping it against his.

The ceremony was boring for both of them, but the sailing coach from Duke was a nice guy and Sam liked him. Sam applauded when Macy went to accept the trophy for second place. Macy flashed him a smile when Sam stood and pulled out her chair.

Her coach took the trophy and smiled. "You two should get out of here," he whispered. "Go; enjoy the rest of the weekend."

Macy glanced at Sam. "Let's go," she whispered.

A few minutes later they were in Sam's truck and driving toward the house. The music was loud and there were people everywhere. By the time they reached the stairs, both had been handed a beer. She led him upstairs into a bedroom on the second floor.

"We can change in here," she said, locking the door behind them. Sam raised an eyebrow.

Catching his look, she amended the statement. "I'll change in the bathroom and you can change in here."

Sam laughed while she walked toward a closed door. "You sure?"

"You might want to put on a swimsuit, there's a pool or we can go down to the beach."

He hadn't quite finished pulling up his bathing suit when she came out of the bathroom.

"Oh!" she said looking at him. Sam finished getting his suit on while she turned away. "Sorry, didn't realize you weren't finished."

"Well, now you've seen mine," he said straight faced, "I should get to see yours."

She shook her head and backed toward the bathroom. "It was an accident."

He laughed while she tried in vain to explain. "I'm just kidding," Sam said with a smile. "Unless…"

She pushed him out the door toward the pool. "Have you ever been sailing?" Macy asked while they weaved through the crowd gathered in the house.

"No, but I've always wanted to try it."

She offered him her hand. "Come on then."

They walked onto the beach, where a catamaran was sitting above the tideline.

"Help me get it in the water." Sam and Macy pushed it out into the water, past the breaking waves.

He held the boat still until she could get the sails ready, then gave it a shove and jumped on with her. She explained how the boat worked and showed him how to control the trim of the sails while she sailed them away from the shore. The surface of the water was calm and a light breeze was blowing in toward the shore. He enjoyed watching her maneuver the small craft with grace and confidence. After a little while, she let the wind out of the sails and offered to switch places.

"You want me to sail back?"

"You can do it. Just watch out for the jib-boom when you tack. It can hurt you when it swings."

They traded places and she helped him get settled into a good position at the tiller.

"Now take up the slack in the rope until the sail gets tight, then hold it." Sam worked the rudder and turned back toward the shore. The little boat began to pick up speed across the waves. He trimmed the sails, experimenting with the tension to increase and decrease their speed. Macy explained how to watch the surface of the water to judge the wind direction and speed. Sam was beginning to get the hang of it and she sat back to enjoy the ride. "You're doing really good," she said, encouraging him.

He smiled at her, pleased that she was happy with his novice skills. Under her direction, he was able to bring them back to the beach and land the boat on the sand. She showed him how to drop the sail and tie them down before suggesting they go back to the house.

"Well, now you know what I like to do to relax, what do you do to unwind?"

"I can show you tomorrow, if you aren't busy."

"I don't have anything to do until I leave tomorrow night," a little sadness in her reply.

"You don't sound too happy about leaving."

"I wish I'd met you a few days ago. It's been fun hanging out with you, but the weekend is almost over and I doubt we'll see each other again."

"Raleigh isn't very far. I could come up and visit, if you wanted me to."

"That would be nice, but it's a long drive," she said, making him laugh. They went back to the house and joined the party. They found a spot in the corner of the pool, where he pulled her close and kissed her. They stayed there, arms wrapped around each other, kissing while everyone around them continued to drink and party. Tired from the busy day, yet not wanting the night to end, they exited the water and went inside. She took him to her room, turning on the lamp beside the bed before disappearing into the bathroom. She returned a second later, tossing him a towel, so he could dry off. She wrapped her towel around her shoulders, pulling it tight and shivering. Sam walked over to her and wrapped his arms around her to provide some warmth.

"Is that better?" he asked, enjoying the feel of her in his arms.

She looked up into his eyes and Sam felt his knees grow weak. She released the towel she was holding, letting it fall and placing her hands on his chest. Sam ran his hands down her back, continuing to look into her eyes. Her hands moved up his chest to his neck, then to the back of his head, pulling his face to hers. Sam felt the heat of her kiss and pulled her tightly against him while their tongues intertwined. She ran her hands into his hair, while one of his hands traced up her back to caress her neck. Sam ran his thumb across her cheek while holding her neck. He felt the heat from her body pressed against his, their skin touching everywhere their swimsuits didn't cover. Macy stepped back, breaking their kiss. He saw the desire in her eyes; he knew his was reflected in his own. She pulled him close again, turning him toward the bed, and then pressing against him until she pushed him against the mattress. She broke their kiss again, long enough to push him onto the bed.

"It's time you got to see mine." she told him, taking off her top.

Sam couldn't help but stare at her body. When he looked into her eyes again, he noticed the smile on her lips. She leaned over him, her hands tracing down his chest toward the bathing suit he still wore. Slowly, she untied the knot while his hands softly moved over the curves of her ribs down to her waist. Removing what was left of their swimwear, she joined him in the bed. Their lovemaking was intense and, being a little tipsy from the beer, a little awkward. When they were done, Macy left him to go to the bathroom. Sam waited on her, though he felt exhausted. She returned wearing a tee-shirt and quickly turned out the light. Crawling under the cover with him, she snuggled up next to him and both fell asleep.

They woke in the morning, a little hung over, and decided they needed showers, then breakfast. The house was quiet when they made their way out to his truck and Sam found a place open for breakfast.

"So, Sam, you still haven't told me what you like to do for fun."

"Finish eating and I promise I'll show you." When they were done, he drove through Savannah, Georgia and over into South Carolina. An hour later, in the small town of Ridgeland, he turned into the airport and parked beside a beat up old hangar.

"You fly?"

"I do. I have a couple of planes out here. Would you like to go up?"

"I've only flown once, but that was on a big plane."

"This is a lot different from flying on the big planes. Wait here a second." He unlocked a small side door then pushed the larger hanger doors open. Sitting inside was a red and white Cessna 172 Skyhawk. Beside it sat a small Extra EA-300 painted dark green and white.

"How did you get into flying?"

He opened the cabin door and released the brake on the Cessna. "I rescued a pilot from a plane crash. He taught me how to fly and work on the planes while he recovered. This plane was in bad shape and I asked him about fixing it. He told me if I could get it running and cleaned up enough to pass an FAA inspection, he'd give it to me. I finished it about six months later and he lived up to his word."

He held the door while she climbed into the right seat. Sam used a tow bar on the front wheel to pull the plane out of the hangar. He checked the plane over and climbed into the left seat, providing a headset for her to put on before he donned his own. "Ready?"

She looked a little scared but nodded and he started the engine. The motor came to life immediately with a loud roar before settling into a steady purr. Sam explained the gauges to her while he waited for the engine to warm up. When the plane was ready, he taxied to the end of the runway and stopped to make sure the runway was clear. "Last chance to change your mind." She shook her head and grinned nervously at him. "Then hold on!" He announced their intended departure to other aircraft in the area by radio and then pushed the throttle forward. Accelerating down the runway, they felt the push of gravity against their bodies while the plane gathered enough speed to produce lift. With a gentle hand, he eased the stick back, lifting the aircraft free of the runway.

Climbing to two thousand feet, he called out a visual flight plan to take them over Hilton Head and Tybee islands. He looked over and saw Macy taking in the scenery, a happy grin on her face. He flew along the coast, where she could see people starting to set up little camps for their day on the beach. He flew the length of the two islands then turned back toward Ridgeland.

"Would you like to fly it?"

She looked at him like he was crazy. "I can't fly a plane."

"I couldn't sail a boat until last night. If I can sail, you can fly. You'll be fine, I'll be right here if anything happens."

He walked her through putting her hands on the controls and told her what gauges to keep an eye on. He took his hands off the yoke and watched her fly the course.

"Just make small adjustments. Just like sailing, watch the wind and adjust to maintain your course," he told her when she began to drift a little.

She slowly became comfortable at the controls. He took over again when they approached the airport and Sam brought the plane in for a landing. He taxied back to the hangar and shut down the engine.

"That was fun," she said. "I see why you like it. You were right about it being different from an airliner."

Sam pushed the plane into the hangar and made sure it was secure before closing the doors and locking them.

"Ready to go back or should I show you around town?"

They rode around town for a while and eventually parked at one of the gas stations for Sam to fill up the tank.

"Romeo, you out there?" said a voice over the CB radio in Sam's truck.

Sam picked up the mike as Macy looked at him funny. "This is Romeo, go ahead."

"This is Little Red, what's your 20?"

Sam smiled. "I'm making a fuel stop on the south end of town; you mobile?"

"I'll see you in two minutes." Little Red replied.

Sam set the mike down and Macy asked, "What was that about?"

"Romeo is my handle, but not for the reason you think," he said when she raised an eyebrow at him. "It's the first letter of my last name."

She didn't look convinced. "Little Red is my friend Alex. He drives a little red pickup, hence the call sign. He'll be here in a minute."

"What would my call sign be?" she asked him. He looked at her for a second, thinking.

"I can think of a few names for you. Wild thing is the first that comes to mind." She swatted him on the arm, making him laugh. "I'm kidding," he said, pulling her into a hug which turned into a short kiss. "Blue Devil is too obvious; what about Emerald, the color of your gorgeous eyes?"

"I like it better than your first suggestion," she replied, pouting.

Hearing the truck of his best friend Alex pull into the parking lot, Sam moved his truck away from the pump and parked next to the red Chevy Luv pickup.

"Hey, Sam," Alex said, waiting for Sam to climb out of the truck. He spotted Macy and paused.

"Alex, this is Macy, CB handle 'Emerald'," Sam said with a grin. "Macy, this is my best friend Alex, aka Little Red."

They each said hello and she excused herself to go get something to drink. Alex was instantly curious.

"Dude, she's gorgeous. Where'd you meet her?" he asked when she walked inside. "Does she have any friends?"

"While you were playing in the water, I took a walk. She's part of a sailing team from Duke University and no, her friends aren't with her."

"Did you take her up in the plane yet?" Alex asked with a grin.

Sam nodded. "She took me sailing yesterday, so I returned the favor and took her up in the Cessna."

Macy came out with three drinks and handed one to each before Alex could respond. "Do you have to work tomorrow, Sam?" she asked.

"I don't have to work for two weeks, but I do have a couple of practices." She gave him a funny look. "I was thinking I could stay over another day, if you wouldn't mind flying me back to Raleigh. I could show you around campus, you could stay with me at the apartment."

Sam smiled at the idea and looked at his buddy. "What do you think about a road trip?"

Chapter 2

The swells were starting to pick up and the old man noticed a line of squalls building off the coast of Argentina closing rapidly on his port side. Thunder crashed in the distance, a deep bass roll predicting rough weather to come. He made good time so far and in a few more hours, he would be back in his beloved Caribbean Ocean. He wasn't sure exactly why he loved those waters more than the rest; he just knew he felt different once he reached them. A gust of wind hit his craft without warning and tipped the sailboat precariously on its side. Cursing his lapse of attention, he tacked to starboard to use the gust for a small speed boost. The wind was being fickle and eased before trying to surprise him again with another burst. He checked his sails and decided to cut back on his canvas so the wind pushing the clouds didn't roll his boat over. It would mean sacrificing some speed, but improved his safety margin. He set the autopilot then clipped himself to the lifeline and headed slowly toward the front of the boat to lower one of the sails. He went about his chore thinking of his past again.

Sam refueled his plane for the flight to Raleigh. Alex sat in the back, leaving Sam to work the radio and navigate. During the two-hour flight, Alex told Macy stories from Sam's past, making sure to include the ones about every girlfriend he'd ever had.

"Alex, old buddy, I hope you brought your running shoes, 'cause when we land, you're gonna need 'em."

Macy laughed at him. "We all have a past, what matters is the present."

Not long after they were on the ground, Macy called her parents to let them know she was back in town and tell them about the competition. Sam returned to the plane to secure it while she talked on the pay phone with her parents. Alex hung out, waiting on the two of them to decide what they were doing next. Sam rejoined them a few moments before she hung up.

"Good news, my parents have invited us to dinner tonight."

"Count me out. I'll find something around here, meeting the parents isn't my thing. I'm going to catch a cab somewhere I can find dinner and a movie. I'll meet you at the hotel outside the airport when you're done," Alex said when they stopped at the rental car counter. They picked up a small car, loaded their bags in the trunk, and drove nearly an hour outside the city to the McCoy family farm. Sam stopped in front of the house, a little intimidated by the size of their home. The house was a colonial style mansion with four large columns across the front of two stories of red brick. Large bay windows on the first floor faced the immaculately manicured lawn, complete with topiaries leading up the walk to the front door.

"This is where you live?"

"Why, is there something wrong with it?" she asked.

"No, it's just not what I was expecting when you said your family owned a farm."

Macy laughed, leading him up the walk to the front door. "Come on, I want you to meet my parents. They're going to love you."

Her parents were nice, and over dinner Sam learned the history of her family. Macy's father, George McCoy, had started out growing tobacco. He made a small fortune on the farm, bought more land, which made more money. He'd married well, adding to his good fortune; she was the daughter of one of Raleigh's oldest families, Sophie Simpson, Macy's mother. Their three boys had studied business, law and medicine and lived nearby, working in the city. Macy's father doted on her and shared her love of the water. George bought the family a summer house in the Outer Banks where her dad and Uncle Jack took her sailing for the first time at the age of eight. Macy had fallen in love with sailing and her father bought a small sailboat. The dinner was going well until George asked what Sam's father did for a living.

"He works in construction."

"Please leave me his card. I might have some work for a good construction contractor."

Sam realized he misunderstood. "He's a plumber for a construction company, sir. My mom teaches fourth and fifth grade at a small school back home."

There was a long silence after his announcement. "What college are you attending?" Sophie McCoy asked, changing the subject.

Sam took a swallow of water before answering. "I'm not attending college. I'm a pilot; I fly air shows around the country."

There was a pleasant smile from each of them, Sam could see right through.

"Sam owns his own plane, he restored it himself. He was nice enough to fly me home after Dean left me on Tybee," Macy said, seeing the looks on her parent's faces.

Her father looked at her and smiled. "We're thankful you're home and safe," he said kindly.

Macy didn't live with her parents; they purchased an apartment for her close to the campus, which she shared with her friend, Timber. They left the McCoy's and made the hour-long trip to her apartment, picking up Alex on the way.

Timber was sitting at her computer when they walked in. Alex immediately went to check out both the machine and the girl. Timber was nice and took an immediate liking to Alex.

"Sorry about tonight," she told Sam when they were alone.

"It's not the first time a girl's parents didn't like me."

"Usually they aren't so critical, but you're the first guy I've brought home they didn't pick for me."

"You aren't betrothed to anyone are you?" he asked, making her laugh.

"No."

"Good, I don't want to be forced into a duel over you. I'd hate to have to kill someone."

"They're not that old fashioned, they're just protective."

"I'm just glad my clothes didn't catch fire after the roasting they gave me."

"I should probably check on Timber and Alex," she said, changing the subject.

She opened the door to her room while Sam followed her. They saw Timber and Alex sitting on the couch kissing.

"Maybe we should talk to him tomorrow," Sam whispered in her ear.

He flew two air shows before his next weekend off, and Sam flew to Raleigh. Macy met him at the airport and took him back to her place. They left a trail of clothes leading to her room, unable to keep their hands off each other. Lying beside him while catching their breath, Macy had an idea.

"We should fly out to the beach. Uncle Jack called and the sailboat's ready, all we have to do is get to *Kill Devil*. He said we could have it for the weekend."

"Sounds like a great idea, we can leave first thing in the morning."

They were up early the next morning and off to the airport for the two-hour flight to the outer banks of North Carolina. Macy's Uncle Jack met them at the airport and took them on another two-hour trip down the coast to Hatteras Island, where the McCoy family beach house sat. During the drive, Jack discovered Sam was a pilot, he asked him a thousand questions about flying.

"I would be glad to take you up some time," Sam offered.

"I'll hold you to that."

The McCoy family beach house was a large two-story house built on stilts. Getting out of the car, Sam could smell the scents of salt air and suntan lotion on the breeze. Jack and his family were staying at the house for the weekend and Sam got to meet them for the first time. Jack's wife, Lynn, was easy going and their two kids, Mike and Mark, liked Sam immediately. Macy showed him around the house, and then took him out to the back yard. Across the lawn was a dock with a sailboat tied to it. The boat was a small 24-foot sailboat with a sleeper cabin, seating area, and galley.

"Have you sailed before?" Jack asked Sam.

"Once, but it was a much smaller boat."

"Well, Macy's a great one to learn from. She can make this boat fly in the lightest of breezes."

Sam and Macy took their bags onboard and got everything ready to go. "We'll be back late tonight or tomorrow, depending on the wind and tide," Macy told her uncle.

She started the small motor used for docking and steered away from the dock. She used the time to instruct Sam how to raise and lower the sails. He learned how to keep one eye on the jib so it didn't knock him overboard. Sam was a quick study and was soon anticipating her commands from the wheel. They dropped anchor in a protected place known as West Bluff Bay where they spent the afternoon swimming and exploring the shore, and the night in each other's arms, watching the ghost crabs walking the shore in the moonlight. It was before dawn the next morning when Sam woke. He fixed coffee and she joined him by the wheel to watch the sun rise.

"I wish I could just sail off with you," she commented after a long silence.

Sam put his arm around her. "Yeah, we could head south and become pirates, looting our way through the Caribbean."

"Captain Emerald McCoy and her trusty first mate Romeo?" she asked with a gleam in her eye.

"Aye, aye, Captain."

Macy shook her head slowly. "What would we tell our parents?"

"We can send them a post card from paradise saying, 'Wish you were here, but please don't visit'," she laughed. "That would make my dad happy. He's already after me to start helping on the farm next summer. Mom's just as bad; I swear she's invited all of their friends with sons my age over for dinner in the last two weeks."

Sam watched a couple of birds riding on a current of air. "I don't think your parents like me much."

"It doesn't matter what they think. It only matters what I think, and I think I love you."

Sam looked at her to find her watching him for his reaction. He smiled, seeing she meant what she'd said and feeling his heart leap. "I love you, too."

The smile crossing her face made the rising sun seem dull by comparison. She pulled his face to hers for a long kiss, making them miss the sunrise. When they parted, their smiles seemed permanently etched in place. Macy leaned her head on his shoulder, content to just be held by him, while Sam wished he could freeze time and stay here forever. After a quick snack for breakfast, they began their journey back to the beach house.

They were met on the dock by Uncle Jack who helped secure the boat. "Your mom's looking for you. She called twice last night and again this morning."

She nodded, checking Sam's knots and gathering her bags before walking up the dock to return her mother's call. Jack took Sam toward the garage to show him the motorcycle he kept there, and to talk.

"I take it my brother doesn't like you very much, Sam."

Sam looked at him, not knowing where he was going with the question. "Don't worry, I love my brother. But he's forgotten where he came from. I'm not going to tell him what you think of him." Sam shrugged his shoulders. "He hasn't liked me since he learned that I'm just a commoner."

Jack laughed. "That's a good way to put it. George isn't bad; he just wants what's best for his daughter. I'm not saying he's right, I just want you to understand how he thinks."

"If he's worried about me being able to take care of her, then he's way off base. I make eight thousand dollars a show, after I've taken care of the maintenance and fuel. I pay rent on a trailer I share with a friend. The promoter takes care of the hotel rooms; on the road, all I have to cover is my meals. I make more money than my parents and they've worked a lot longer than I have."

Jack grinned. "I didn't know you did shows."

"I fly aerobatic competitions and air shows around the country. Your brother heard that and turned his nose up faster than if I had taken a crap on his dinner plate."

Jack burst out laughing at the comment. "If you're serious about her, let me talk to him. Lynn thinks the two of you make a cute couple, so she's also on your side."

They rejoined the rest of the family and found Macy and Lynn in the kitchen having what looked to be the same conversation. "Is everything alright with your mom?" Sam asked, standing next to Macy.

"She was wondering where I was, because she wanted me to come over for dinner again," she said, rolling her eyes. "When she called the apartment, Timber told her I was coming here and she wanted to know what I was doing." Sam remained quiet and let her vent.

"You're welcome to stay here with us if you want," Lynn told them. "There's plenty of room."

Macy looked at Sam. "What do you think?"

"Whatever you want to do, Captain."

Sam's next show was a Labor Day show in Wilmington that would be capped off by the Blue Angels. He set aside tickets for Macy, Jack's family and Macy's parents. He had them cleared into the VIP area so they could see how he lived while he was on the road. Sam flew Jack's family and Macy down to Wilmington for the show a day before the practice session and got them in to watch a practice. Sam introduced Macy to the pilots he flew with and they couldn't resist trying to embarrass him in front of her. Sam called in a favor from one of the Blue Angel pilots and got Jack a ride in the back of an F-18. Jack grinned the rest of the day and couldn't stop talking about it.

The following day, Macy got to see Sam perform his show for the first time. His flying was near perfect, knowing that she was watching him and wanting to impress her. After he landed, Sam spent a lot of time signing autographs while he walked along the line of spectators at the edge of the field. By the time he finished, the Blue Angels were about to fly. He walked back and found Macy so they could watch the show together.

"These guys are what inspired me to want to do this."

"You were wonderful up there."

He grinned at her and gave her a quick kiss before her cousins Mike and Mark came up, followed by Jack and Lynn.

"That was a great show, Sam," the two boys said, replaying his flight with their hands. The boys were ages 11 and 8 and believed Sam could do no wrong. Jack quieted them when the Angels began their show.

Sam couldn't help but smile watching them fly. He laughed at the whole family when the solo jets performed their "sneak pass", making them wonder where they came from. When the show was over and the Angels were waiting for their planes to be refueled, Sam got them to take a picture with Jack and his family. Once they were back at the motel and changed, Jack insisted on taking everyone out for dinner. Sam noticed Macy was quiet during dinner, but when he asked her what was wrong, she changed the subject. After dinner, they went back to the motel and Jack said goodnight to them in the hall. Jack gave Macy a look Sam caught, but no one said anything. Jack held out his hand to Sam.

"Thanks for everything, Sam. You've made me and the boys lifelong fans of air shows."

Sam laughed and told him to rest because they were going again the next day. Jack just grinned and headed into his room, leaving Macy and Sam alone in the hall. "You've been kind of quiet tonight," Sam said after they walked into her room.

She sat on the edge of the bed and looked at the floor. "Sorry, I didn't mean to be bad company."

He leaned down and kissed her on the head. "You weren't, but I could tell something's bothering you."

"I should've known you'd pick up on it. I'm furious with my parents."

"Why?"

"You invited them to the show and they ignored your invitation. I was worried we might have missed them, so I called to make sure they were alright. Mom said Wilmington was too far away and they had plans with friends."

"Did you talk to Jack about it?"

"Yeah, Uncle Jack talked to Daddy, who made it clear he wasn't coming and you were just after our money." Sam was surprised. "Uncle Jack was angrier than I'd ever seen him."

Sam was quiet for a moment. "I'm sorry for all this."

She turned to him and shook her head. "There is nothing for you to be sorry for. None of this is your fault. You've been nothing but generous to everyone. Uncle Jack was so happy today, he was about to explode. Aunt Lynn told me she'd only seen him like that three other times; their wedding, and when the boys were born."

"I still feel bad for causing trouble in your family."

She laid back on the bed and put her hand on his back. "Let's not worry about it right now. You were amazing up there today. I didn't know someone could fly an airplane like that."

"I think it was my best show yet, mostly because I was trying to impress you."

"Know what the best part was?

Sam shook his head.

"It was seeing all of those girls throwing themselves at you and knowing I was the one you were going home with."

Sam took them back to Raleigh on Sunday night. He said goodbye to Jack and his family at the terminal. "Put in a good word for me with the family, I think I'll need it."

"Don't worry about that old windbag brother of mine. Dad's the real force in this family and Macy's his favorite. I'll talk to him and have him straighten out my fool brother."

"Thanks, Jack, for everything." Macy told them goodbye and led Sam over to where Timber was supposed to be meeting her. "When will you be back?"

Sam's schedule for the next three months was booked solid and most of his shows were in the Midwest. "If nothing changes in the schedule, I'll see you around Thanksgiving."

She looked sad at the news. "I'm going to miss you," she said, holding onto him tightly.

He put his arms around her and held her close, trying to remember her smile and the smell of her perfume.

"I'll talk to you every time I get a chance."

Timber pulled up before she could answer and blew the horn. "Welcome home," Timber shouted.

Sam kissed Macy goodbye before she got in the car to leave. "It won't be that long until I get back."

"It'll be too long, I already miss you."

Sam watched her drive away and waved until they were out of sight.

The time passed slowly and during the month of September they traded phone calls each week. They had a difficult time connecting with each other at the beginning of November and Sam was worried something was wrong. His last two shows were canceled due to bad weather and he caught a redeye flight to Raleigh, leaving his crew to get the plane back to South Carolina. He caught a cab to Macy's apartment, planning on staying the last two weeks leading up to Thanksgiving. Timber answered the door, surprised to see him.

"You weren't due back for two more weeks," she said leaving him standing in the hall.

"My last two shows were cancelled so I came back early. Where's Macy, I wanted to surprise her."

Timber tried to give him a blank look. "I don't know."

Sam knew something was definitely wrong. "Timber, you're a terrible liar. I've been in the air for the last eight hours. I'm tired, hungry and not in the mood for games. Where is she?"

Timber pulled the door open and let him in. "You'd better come inside." Sam walked inside and waited for her to answer his question. She looked at him for a moment trying to decide what to do.

"She didn't tell me where she was going. She was upset and told me that she would be back in a couple of days."

Sam wondered what could have upset her so much that she would leave in the middle of a semester. "Do you know what she was upset about?"

"She didn't say, she just left," Timber told him. "You could try her parents' house; they might know where she is."

"I don't think they'd give me the time of day, much less tell me where I can find their daughter." Then he had an idea. "Do you have her Uncle Jack's number?"

Timber said Macy kept a list of numbers by the phone in the kitchen. Sam went into the kitchen and found the list. A moment later he was listening to the phone ring and hoping Jack would answer.

"Hello?" Jack answered.

"Jack? It's Sam, I'm looking for Macy. Do you know where she is?"

Jack was quiet for a moment. "Sam, I'm surprised you called, considering what you've done.

Sam was confused. "What are you talking about?"

"She saw the picture of you kissing the little blonde girl. How could you do that to her?"

Sam let out a frustrated breath. "Jack, I really don't know what you're talking about. I haven't kissed anyone since I told Macy goodbye. If I could talk to her or see her, I might be able to explain."

Jack was quiet for a moment. "Don't let her know how you found out, but she's at the beach house. Her mom took her there to help her sort out her feelings."

"Thanks, Jack."

Sam asked Timber if she would take him to a car rental place and an hour later, he was driving east toward the coast. It was almost two in the morning when he arrived at the beach house. He considered sleeping in the car until he remembered the sailboat. Sam parked the car where it wouldn't get towed and slipped over the fence surrounding the property. He climbed onboard the boat and went to the cabin to rest. He lay down on the bed and was soon asleep, despite the swirl of questions going through his mind. Somewhere in his dreams he heard Macy's voice. It wasn't until he heard the thump of a footstep on the boat that he realized she was onboard.

"Mom, I can run the boat by myself, I've done it before." Macy was saying. "I'll be fine; I just need some time to think some things through. I'll be back tomorrow."

Sam couldn't hear what her mother said in return, but he heard the engine start and her moving around on the deck, untying the boat from the dock. Sam stayed where he was and waited until he could feel the boat moving before getting out of bed. The engine shut off and she began moving around the deck again, setting the sails. He walked out onto the deck and waited for her to return to the cockpit.

"Oh!" she said, spotting him on her way back. "Where did you come from and how'd you get onboard?"

"My last two shows were cancelled and I came back to see you. You weren't at your apartment and Timber said you left, upset about something," he said while she took her place at the wheel. "I figured you would come here to get away and think, so I drove five hours, after an eight-hour flight, to find you. I didn't think you wanted me to wake you up at two in the morning, so I came here to get some sleep." She refused to look at him, staring instead at the water in front of them. "You don't look too happy to see me," he said, testing her mood.

"I'm not; in fact, I really didn't ever want to see you again."

He felt a pain in his heart at her words. "Why? I love you and you said you loved me. What changed?"

She gave him a look that could freeze water. "I saw the picture of you and some blonde girl kissing. How could I have been so stupid to believe you when you cared so little for me? Why would you kiss her if you loved me? You get lonely on the road or do you keep a girl in every city?"

Sam looked at her for a moment. "What are you talking about?"

She opened her purse and took out a picture. "This is what I'm talking about," she said, shoving the picture at him. In the picture was Sam and a blonde in skin-tight leather racing suit, kissing each other in front of a sign from the Mirage hotel in Las Vegas. In the corner of the picture was the date October 25th. "I hope she was worth it, because once we get back, I never want to see you again." She spun the wheel, making him duck to avoid the jib-boom.

Sam offered her the picture back. "Keep it," she told him.

Sam watched her at the wheel for a moment. "Would you like an explanation, or are you just going to keep hating me?"

She gave him another dirty look. "Why should I believe anything you have to say?"

"Because I've never lied to you. The picture is real, and yes, I did kiss the girl, her name was Danielle. I met her at the aerobatic competition in Las Vegas last year, after I won the event. The picture was taken during the award dinner and I can prove it."

Macy watched him for a moment. "You're telling me this is a picture from last year?"

"The date was changed on this one to match up with the competition this year, in case you checked. The competition last year was in October, but it was on the sixteenth not the twenty-fifth. I have a copy of a newspaper article that was written about it and the date is on the trophy. I can show you both of them to prove my innocence."

She didn't say anything for a few minutes. She let out a long breath and suddenly turned the boat hard, setting it on a course back to the beach house. "You have one chance to prove you're telling the truth. If you're lying to me, I'll see to it you're made as miserable as I've been the last two weeks."

When they reached the house, Macy took him inside. Her mom was furious to find Sam there and threatened to have him arrested for stalking and trespassing. Macy stopped her from calling the police for a few minutes.

Macy looked at him. "Prove you're not lying, or go to jail."

He smiled, asking her to pick up the phone and listen while he picked up a different one and started dialing a number from memory. Sam talked to his mom and asked her to find both the article and the trophy. When she had both, he asked her to read the dates off each one.

"The trophy says October 16, 1989, and the article is dated the day after," she told him.

"Thanks, you just helped me settle a disagreement over the dates," he said, before saying he'd see her in a couple of weeks and hanging up. Sam looked across the kitchen at Macy where she'd been listening to the conversation. Slowly she set the phone down and raised her head. Tears were pouring down her face.

"That's what I thought," her mother said smugly. "I'll call Chief Dandridge and have him removed immediately."

Macy ignored her and focused on Sam. "Please forgive me for doubting you."

Sam went to her and wrapped her in a big hug. "There's nothing to forgive."

"How can you let him touch you after what he's done? Do you need to see the picture of him kissing that hideous girl to remind you?"

Macy turned to her and shook her head. "Mom, it was a picture from an event last year, before we met."

Her mother was speechless for a moment, but recovered quickly. "Why, because one of his friends told you? Are you so foolish to believe that he wouldn't call them just to tell you what you wanted to hear?"

Macy's anger toward Sam was redirected at her mother. "The person he called had no idea what was happening and he didn't tell them. He just asked them to give him a date from two items, they did; proving he was right," she said hotly.

Her mother laughed at her. "And exactly how do you know this person wasn't trying to keep their job with him?"

"Because it was his mother!" she shouted. Mrs. McCoy stood there shocked.

Sam wasn't sure if it was the fact that Macy had yelled at her or that his mom had been the one who had straightened things out; but Mrs. McCoy was at a loss for words.

"Come on, Sam, you can help me pack, then take me home," Macy said, leading him out of the room.

The packing took a little longer because of all of the kissing they did until her mom showed up to help. There was an obvious strain between Mrs. McCoy and Sam, making him wonder if she wasn't the one behind Macy finding the picture. Sam wished he had brought his plane because of the long drive ahead of them. They were both tired, but happy to be together again. They finally decided to stop and get a room where they could catch a few hours of sleep and fool around a little before finishing their trip. The next morning, they resumed their trip back to Raleigh. Though her parents tried to call several times, she refused to talk to them. Timber ran interference for her until the semester ended on Friday. The only person in her family she cared about talking to was her Uncle Jack, who confessed to telling Sam where she went. Her brothers had stopped by and treated Sam well, but she told them she refused to talk to their parents. Sam invited her to go home and share Thanksgiving with him and his family. She agreed, so Sam made the arrangements for them to fly to Charleston where his younger brother would pick them up. Macy had met his parents briefly when he had taken her flying for the first time, but she never met his brother Trey. She laughed at how much they looked alike.

"People tell us that all the time," Trey said. "I think I look better though."

Sam laughed. "Maybe in your dreams."

She spent the two weeks leading up to Thanksgiving at the trailer Sam shared with Alex. She met half of his family when they all got together at his grandmother's house to eat. Much to the delight of his grandmother, Macy volunteered to help with the cleaning while Sam was sent outside with his cousins to talk and catch up. In the quiet time after the big meal, Sam showed her the scrapbook his mom made of his shows and competitions. She saw all of his trophies and even looked through his pictures from different shows.

She finally called home, from the phone in his room, to wish them a Happy Thanksgiving and talked with her grandfather.

On Sunday afternoon, she said goodbye to his family and Sam flew her home.

While putting the plane to bed in the hanger, she announced, "I need to go see my family. I've never been away from them during the holidays and Grandpa's upset."

"Do you want me to come along for moral support?"

She gave him a smile, making him feel warm inside. "Thanks, you're sweet, but I think I'll do this on my own. I'll be back in a few hours."

Sam hung out there at her apartment by himself while she went to her parent's house. Just as he found a football game to watch, the phone rang. He'd never answered her phone and wasn't about to now. He waited for the answering machine to pick up, while he went to pour another glass of sweet tea. Just after the message played on the answering machine and the beep went off, he heard Macy's voice over the phone.

"Sam if you're there, please pick up," He grabbed the phone and stopped the recording.

"Hey, what's up?"

"What were you doing?" she asked.

"I was watching a football game and fixing something to drink."

"My grandpa wants to meet you and Uncle Jack's on his way to pick you up. He'll be there in an hour."

Sam let out a long breath. "How do your parents feel about me coming over there?"

"Grandpa told them he wanted to meet this boy who had caused so much strife and made his favorite grandchild miss Thanksgiving dinner with him."

Sam let out a groan. "Great, another member of your family that thinks I'm trouble."

She was quick to reply. "He isn't angry with you; he just wants to meet you. I really want you to meet him, he used to fly, too."

Sam showered and changed into some nice clothes before meeting Jack in front of her building. The ride was fun and Sam liked Jack's red Porsche a lot. "So, daddy wants to meet you? This could be really good or really bad," Jack teased.

Sam shook his head. "You and Lynn are the only ones in the family besides her brother Dan who'll even speak to me," Sam held on while Jack zipped around a tight corner. "I could understand if I looked like you or smelled bad, but I don't."

Jack laughed, "Keep it up and there will be one less McCoy on your side. Don't worry, Dad's more like me than George. Mom is just like any other Grandma, she loves everybody. Just treat them like you treat me and you'll be fine."

Sam laughed. "I think I'll treat him better than that."

They arrived at the house and Macy met them in the yard. Sam was suddenly nervous about meeting the man she cared so much for. She took him into the house and to the den where her grandfather was watching TV. The old man focused on him from the moment he walked through the door. He had the same shade of green eyes Macy had but his seemed to burn into Sam while he studied him.

"Grandpa, this is Sam Richards," Macy said introducing them. "Sam, this is my Grandpa McCoy." Sam shook the old man's hand firmly.

"Nice to meet you, sir."

Sam estimated the man was in his mid-seventies but his handshake was like iron. He was thin but not frail. And there was no doubt from his bearing that his word was law.

"Have a seat, son." Macy started to sit with them but he stopped her. "Honey, go find your Grandma and ask her to join us."

She popped up and rushed out the door after giving Sam's hand a squeeze. George was sitting in his chair watching the two of them with interest. "George, could you give me a few minutes with this young man? I have a few things to talk to him about."

George nodded, "Yes, sir." He got up, casting an evil smile at Sam before leaving the two of them alone in the room.

The old man pushed a button on the remote and turned off the TV. He looked at Sam intently.

"Son, you've caused quite a stir in this house. I've heard two different opinions of you from my boys and I wanted to judge for myself." He watched Sam as he spoke and Sam felt the weight of his stare. "My granddaughter is quite taken with you. I'm sure you've heard she is considered to be my favorite, though it's only partially true. She's pretty, smart, and will inherit millions on her twenty-first birthday, so I understand my son's reluctance to accept you."

Sam was surprised to hear she would be a millionaire when she turned twenty-one and it showed on his face. "Sir, when I met Macy, I had no idea who she was or if she had a dime. I saw a beautiful girl who was smart, funny and liked the water. Until you just told me about it, I never knew about her inheritance and I don't care. I make enough of my own money that I don't need hers. If I could get her father to understand that, maybe he could get over his mistrust of me and we could make peace."

The old man was quiet for a long moment. "What about her schooling? She should finish college; she has a bright future ahead of her."

Sam nodded. "I agree. Mr. McCoy, she's a gifted woman and I'd never ask her to give up her dreams for me, even if it meant losing her. I don't want her to have any regrets about what she does with her life."

"So, Mr. Richards, what do you do, that makes you so much money?"

Sam smiled proudly. "I'm a pilot and I fly aerobatic planes in air shows."

"That explains why Jack likes you. Macy told me you owned your own plane, but she left out a few details I see."

"She told me you once flew too."

"I did, but it was a long time ago, during the war," Mr. McCoy looked him in the eye. "Son, I'm sorry for grilling you the first time we met. I've always handled problems straight on. I just don't want to see my son or my granddaughter hurt."

"Neither do I, sir."

The door to the room opened and Macy walked in with a woman who looked Sam over critically. Sam endured another session of questions ranging from where he was from to what his family did for a living. Macy got to stay for this round of questions and at the end she looked at her Grandpa for his opinion. "Grandpa, what do you think of him?" she asked bluntly. The old man looked at her and chuckled, while his wife laughed out loud.

"She is more like you than any of the boys."

Mr. McCoy grunted, a small grin growing on his face.

"If you must know what I think of this young man, I'll tell you," he said looking at Sam. "He sat here for the better part of an hour being grilled like a prisoner of war, but not once has he been anything other than polite and honest. I think he's a fine young man and I approve."

Macy looked at her Grandma, who grinned at her and winked. "If you don't want him, I'll trade you this one for him."

Chapter 3

He felt a splash of rain hit his face and reached under his seat for the rain suit he kept there. The sea began to churn, with the swells growing in height and whitecaps forming on the crests. For a moment, he forgot about the green-eyed girl and her family. He watched the cold front approach with a sense of awe, and once again he marveled at the power contained in a storm. A gust of wind tore at his rain coat and staggered him. He saw a flash of lightning and began to count slowly until he heard the thunder roll, three seconds meant three miles until the worst part arrived. He checked the GPS and noted his position before switching it off to save some battery power in case his generator flooded. He checked the sails again and adjusted his course to bring the bow into the wind a bit. He felt the drop in temperature when the front passed, appearing to push the blue sky and sun away in the strong winds. Thunder rolled again and this time the count was down to just under two seconds. With the thunder came the rain; falling in big heavy drops, still cold from their journey from the cloud tops, thousands of feet above. He heard the flapping sound of the sails and quickly tightened the trim. Another strong blast of wind drove the rain into him hard enough to make it sting his exposed, weathered skin. Knowing he was in for a long afternoon and possibly a long night, he rechecked his safety line, put on a life jacket and went forward to make sure the sail locker was fully closed. He learned a long time ago to not take little things for granted on the water. He closed all of the hatches while working his way back to the cockpit, and with a critical eye he mentally checked each item again to make sure he didn't miss anything. With nothing to do but conserve his energy for the coming battle with Mother Nature, he thought back to more of his time with her.

It was her senior year of college and graduation was closing in fast. She was now the captain of the sailing team and under her leadership it had become one of the toughest teams to beat. Sam again stood on the beach at Tybee and watched the regatta, but this time he knew what he was watching and who he was pulling for. He had arranged to have the weekend off so he could pull for Macy to win the last event of the season and they could spend their third anniversary together. He'd told her that morning he had a surprise for her after the regatta. He'd expected her to be excited, but she only smiled sadly.

"We need to talk later," she told him, turning away and leaving him concerned.

Macy had chosen a girl to help her in the race. Sam watched them take a small lead at the first turn and by the second turn they pulled to a three-boat lead over the team from East Carolina University. The Duke team pulled to a larger lead by the time they crossed the finish line and were quickly surrounded by people patting them on the shoulder when they pulled into the shore. Sam stayed back and let the crowd thin before approaching them.

"Good race," he said, forcing a laugh from Macy.

The comment had become a tradition for them when she finished a race. She hugged him and then took off for the tent to sign the time card for the event. With the race done and her boat packed up, Sam took her over to Thunderbolt, Georgia, and pulled into a marina.

"What are we doing here?" she asked when she got out of his truck.

"Follow me and find out," he said, leading her toward the docks where they wound through the ranks of fishing boats and small yachts. "Close your eyes and take my hands." She looked at him funny, making him laugh. "You'll have to trust me." Slowly she held out her hands and put them in his. "Close your eyes, I promise not to let you fall into the water."

He took her out to the very end of the dock and stopped.

"Alright, you can open your eyes now."

Sam stepped aside and watched her face when she looked past him at the surprise he had for her. Sitting at the dock was a fifty-two foot sailboat painted white with green trim.

"Happy graduation and anniversary!"

"What?" she asked when what he said had finally sunk in.

Proudly Sam explained. "This is yours; I bought it for you as an anniversary present and for your graduation from college."

She tore her wide eyes away from the boat long enough to look at him.

"I can't accept this, Sam."

"Why not?" he asked, a little hurt that she wasn't more excited.

"We need to talk."

Sam stepped aboard the boat and she joined him. He sat at the wheel and waited for her to say whatever was on her mind. She stood across the cockpit from him and collected her thoughts.

"Sam, this has been fun, but I've been thinking a lot lately about us and life after graduation. You have a successful career flying and you love what you do. I'm just starting out and I want to make my mark on the world. I should've told you this a week ago, but I've been offered a job in Costa Rica, which I accepted. I leave in a month."

Sam felt like he had been kicked in the gut. For a few seconds, he forgot to breathe while the words of her confession assaulted his mind. He blinked, clearing away his tears and the thought of losing her. He summoned a smile through his heartache, determined to be happy for her sake.

"That's great news, I'm happy for you."

She looked into his eyes seeing the hurt he was trying to hide, behind his smile.

"Sam this wasn't an easy decision and I've been trying to wait for a good time to tell you. We've both been so busy and we haven't seen much of each other lately. Thank you for so thoughtful a gift, but I can't accept this, even though it's beautiful."

He looked at her for a long moment, understanding she was breaking up with him. "I guess this is it then."

She began to cry and wiped her eyes tears rolling down her face.

"Don't cry," Sam said softly, walking over and wrapping his arms around her.

"I'm so sorry," she said through her tears. Sam kissed her on the forehead.

"We'll always have Tybee," he said, changing the line from her favorite movie. She smiled through her tears.

"Here's looking at you, kid. The boat is still yours. You'll need somewhere to live while you're down there, so take it with you."

"I can't. I'll be living on a research vessel for eight months out of the year; I won't have any time to go sailing." She moved away from him. "Could you take me back to the house now?"

He nodded mutely. After locking up the boat, they walked in silence back to where the truck was parked. He drove her back to the rental house on Tybee and stopped in the driveway.

"Are you coming inside?" she asked.

He looked away, trying to hide his broken heart. "I don't think that would be a good idea."

She wiped at her eyes and tried to smile. "I understand. I hope we can stay in touch, I would really like to hear from you now and then."

Sam nodded. "Sure, you know how to get in touch with me, let me know when you get back to the States. If I'm in town, we can catch up and maybe get some dinner sometime."

She nodded silently and opened the door. "Goodbye, Sam, I'll always love you."

She didn't wait for a reply and shut the door before he could reply. He watched her disappear inside the house, wondering if he should try to change her mind. His words to her grandfather echoed in his mind and he let out a long breath. No, it was probably better to just let go and hope that one day they would find their way back to each other. With a heart full of sadness, he backed out and drove away.

Two days later, he received a phone call from the harbormaster at the marina in Thunderbolt.

"Sir, the boat is still here and I have the keys in my possession. The title is listed in your name, but there has been no activity on the boat and there is no agreement in place for us to keep it here."

Sam thanked him explaining he would make sure it was moved by the end of the week. He and Alex headed over to the marina later that afternoon and Sam stopped by the office to pick up the keys.

"That's a fine sailboat you have there, but you know it's bad luck not to give her a name," the guy told him.

"I don't think my luck can get much worse, but why chance it. Do you know someone who can paint a name on for me?"

The man gave Sam a number to call and Sam thanked him again. He met Alex outside and they headed down the dock to where the boat was tied. Sam felt the sadness return when he rounded the corner and saw the boat sitting there.

"You alright?" Alex asked.

Sam climbed aboard, ignoring the question. There was a green ribbon tied around the door to the salon.

"I'll be right back," Sam said, unlocking the door and entering the salon. Inside the boat was warm from being closed for so long. He spotted an envelope sitting on the table with his name written on the front, in Macy's handwriting. He left it on the table and opened all the vents to cool off the inside. He'd left her a vase with a dozen roses on the table, another surprise for her when she went to look around the inside; but they'd never made it inside. The vase was gone but a single, shriveled rose was lying next to his letter. Swallowing the lump in his throat, he sat down and opened the letter.

> *Dear Sam,*
>
> *I just wanted to tell you one more time how sorry I am we didn't work out. The last three years were the happiest of my life and I wouldn't trade them for anything. I know you're hurting as much as I am and I sincerely hope you can someday forgive me for leaving. Please know, wherever you go, you'll take my heart with you. I'll always think of you when I see a plane and I hope you'll remember me when you see the ocean. Every sailor needs a boat and I have mine at the beach house. I want you to have this one as a reminder of the times we shared together; so you can escape when you feel down. Stay safe on your travels and keep in touch, I may have lost you as a lover, but I would die if I lost you as a friend.*
>
> *Love always,*
>
> *Macy*

P.S. – The roses are beautiful.

He dropped the letter on the table, putting his head in his hands. He felt the hot tears roll down his cheeks, falling on the paper while he cried. He thought he was ready to move on, but he knew now she would always haunt him. She was the first girl he'd ever loved; now she was gone. How was he supposed to turn off what he felt for her? Anger and sorrow battled for his emotions while tears rained on her letter. What was next for him? No woman he'd meet would ever be Macy. Was he doomed to spend his life alone? He was wallowing in his misery when he heard Alex's footsteps on the deck. Sam wiped the tears from his eyes and let out a long breath, fighting to compose himself before Alex reached him. His buddy poked his head through the hatch and looked around.

"Wow, this is nice."

Sam picked up the rose and held it under his nose, while Alex came down the steps and joined him.

"You okay?"

He nodded quietly, not trusting his voice. Sam folded the letter and set the rose on top of it. Sliding out from behind the table and leaving the salon, he dialed the number the harbormaster gave him and talked to the man on the other end. Fifteen minutes later the man appeared and Sam told him what he wanted on the stern and how he wanted it done.

"I'll get right to work, sir," the man said.

Sam paid the harbormaster through the rest of the week and asked him if he could get a hook up for power and water. He sent Alex into town to get groceries for a few days.

"Buy enough for yourself, too, if you decide you're coming with me," he told his old friend before he left.

"Where we heading?" Alex asked.

Sam only shrugged. "Where ever the wind takes us."

Chapter 4

The storm was rough and he fought his way up and down the troughs and crests of waves threatening to swamp him. What little light found its way through the thick black clouds faded rapidly when night fell. The old man chuckled, watching a wave brake over the bow sending water across the deck.

I survived worse storms than this. I'll be damned if this is the one that does me in.

He'd reefed his sails earlier to keep them from being blown into shreds and to keep the howling, swirling winds from knocking the boat over. Before the worst of the storm, he poured a large cup of coffee, both to keep him alert and warm in the freezing rain. He'd learned many tricks during his travels and was glad for the warmth the coffee gave his old bones. In the darkness, he was forced to sail by feel and understanding what the water was doing by the way the boat reacted. Forks of lightning arced across the sky and sometimes threw themselves at the water, sending angry geysers into the air. He checked his course again and looked at the clock on the panel in front of him. Waves broke over the bow, sending salty spray through the air, soaking the old man and adding to his misery. The last position check placed him fifty nautical miles south-south-east of Trinidad before the really bad weather caught him. He wanted to reach the leeward side of the island, where he could drop anchor and ride out the rest of the storm. The old man toyed with the idea of turning on the GPS again to check his position, but decided to wait another hour. He did some math on a small calculator and marked a spot on the laminated map beside him. With nothing to do but wait and ride out the gale, his mind wandered back to a different kind of storm.

It was Christmas Eve and he was in Atlanta's Hartsfield International airport, waiting for the weather to change. He was caught with the other holiday travelers, grounded due to an intense winter storm, which dumped eleven inches of snow on the city. He angled into a small bar that was still open and joined the crowd gathered inside. A few merry people were singing Christmas carols to the children who feared Santa wouldn't find them in the airport. Sam found a spot at the bar and ordered a Corona with lime. If he couldn't be in the Caribbean, at least he could drink like he was. The bartender brought over the beer and Sam took a swallow, watching the latest weather report on one of the TVs behind the bar. The weather was expected to clear the next day and flights would resume then. He was deciding what to do next when a voice from the past caught his attention. He looked in the mirror, behind the bartender, to find the source, but it was too crowded. He turned, scanning the faces of the patrons until he found the voice. She was sitting at a table with three men. He watched her a moment, trying to decide what to do. She was still as beautiful as he remembered, though her hair was shorter and her skin darker. She laughed at something one of the men said and for a second, he felt jealous. It had been three years since he'd dropped her off at the house on Tybee. He wrote to her about his shows and travels, leaving out how much he missed her and wanted to see her again; but she had never written back. After a few months, he debated taking the boat and sailing down to Costa Rica to find out why, but he had no idea where to find her. Alex finally talked him out of the idea and told him to give up on her. Somehow, he just couldn't do it. She was like an itch he couldn't reach, slowly driving him mad. He was lost in his thoughts and didn't notice he was still staring at her. One of the men said something to her and she turned to look in his direction. There was a shocked look on her face when she saw him standing at the bar. Without a word to the rest of the people at her table she got up and approached him. Sam watched her walking toward him and noticed she hadn't changed at all. She was still the lithe beauty who had captured his heart long ago. Seeing her now, he realized he still loved her even if she didn't love him.

"Sam?" she asked, walking up to him.

"Macy," he managed to say.

"What in the world are you doing here?"

"I could ask you the same thing; I thought you were in Costa Rica?"

"I got stuck here on my way back to Honduras. My team and I came back to the States for an early Christmas."

He gave her a small smile.

"What about you?"

"I was flying to Norfolk on business," he said simply.

"Why don't you join us? It's not like we're going anywhere right now."

He looked past her at the table and hesitated.

"It looks kind of crowded over there already."

"They're just kissing up to the boss. You shouldn't spend Christmas alone."

He finally agreed and followed her to the table.

"Guys, this is an old friend of mine, Sam Richards. Sam, these are my research assistants, Ryan, Jacob, and John," she said indicating them in turn.

Sam shook hands with them joining the group. He found a chair that was vacant and pulled it next to hers.

"Nice jacket," Ryan said noticing the patches covering his flight jacket. "Are you a pilot?"

Sam nodded.

Macy chuckled. "Sam flies air shows around the country."

They all looked at him to see if she was telling the truth.

"That's where I know you from," John said. "I saw you in New Orleans a year ago. It was your farewell tour, right?"

Sam nodded slowly. "That's right."

Macy looked at him funny. "You don't fly shows anymore?"

Sam shook his head. "No, I got out of it. I do a little promoting when I'm not out sailing and starting a new business."

She looked a little sad at the revelation, but she hid it quickly.

"What kind of research are you doing?" he asked, changing the subject.

The three guys gave him the rundown of their different projects and what they hoped to accomplish. There was an announcement saying all flights were cancelled until the next day and most of the people in the bar began slipping out to find places to sleep for the night.

Sam laughed. "At least I can get into the pilot's lounge to catch a few hours," he said while they started wondering what they were going to do.

"Go outside and find us a taxi. We'll have to find a place to stay for at least one night," Macy instructed her crew.

The three men dropped a few dollars on the table and left the two of them alone for a few minutes.

"I didn't know you stopped flying," she said after an awkward moment.

Sam finished his beer and thoughtfully set the bottle down on the table.

"It was time to move on to other things. After Mom and Dad passed, Alex got married and there wasn't much in it for me anymore,"

She put her hand on his arm. "I didn't know or I would have been there."

He looked into the bottle sitting on the table, fighting the urge to be hateful and remind her it was in the letters she never replied to.

"They were in a car accident. The doc said they went quickly."

"I'm sorry, Sam."

"Like you said, you didn't know. How's your Uncle Jack? I haven't seen him in a long time," Sam said, changing the subject away from him again.

"He's doing fine. You inspired him to finally go and get his pilot's license. He has a Cessna 172 like yours and flies everywhere he can. He even offered to fly us back to Honduras, but Aunt Lynn told him he couldn't."

Sam laughed a little. "How's your grandfather?"

Her smile darkened a little. "He's doing fine but he is getting older and doesn't get around like he used to."

He didn't ask about her parents, mostly because he didn't care how they were doing. Jacob returned and told her they'd found a cab.

"Why don't you join us?" She asked Sam after collecting her things. "I would love to catch up some more."

He thought about it for a second, wondering why she wanted to see him when she'd never replied to his letters. He was about to say no when she smiled at him, changing his mind.

"I guess a motel room is better than a cot."

Her smile widened to a grin and together they walked toward the front door. The five crowded into a small minivan along, with their carry-on luggage. A short ride later, they found themselves at a Comfort Inn where a few rooms were still available.

"I need four rooms," she told the desk clerk.

The woman checked what she had and said. "I only have two available. There's a room with two twin beds and one with a king. That's all we have left."

"Alright then, we'll take them."

The three guys were given the room with the king-sized bed and she and Sam would share the one with the twin beds. The men gave her a strange look before heading up to their room with their luggage.

"Are you up for a little adventure?" she asked Sam after they got on the elevator.

"Adventure is my middle name."

She giggled at his reply. "Your girlfriend isn't going to come and hunt me down is she?" Macy asked, fishing for information.

"I don't have a girlfriend or a wife. I don't need that kind of drama. You?"

"No time for anyone with all of the work I have to do," she replied before the elevator stopped.

Their room was big, with a sitting area separated from the bedroom by a bathroom and a closet. Sam dropped his jacket and backpack in a chair while Macy headed for the bedroom.

"This is cozy," she said looking around the room. "Which side do you want? Window or bathroom?"

"Lady's choice."

She pulled the covers down on the bed closest to the bathroom.

"I'll take this one."

"You can have first shot at the shower, too," he said, turning on the TV.

"There was a time when we used to share a shower," she said.

He looked at her for a moment and she raised her eyebrow at him. "That was a long time ago," he said with a trace of sadness.

She stepped into the bathroom and closed the door without a comment. He suddenly wished he'd stayed at the airport and not put himself through this. Part of him wanted to join her and relive the times they'd shared, but he knew where that would leave him. She'd run off again and he'd still be in love with her and alone. Scooping up his key, he left the room looking for a place to drown his sorrow. He found the small bar they passed on the way to the elevators. The bartender drifted over to him when he sat down.

"You trapped like the rest of them or just don't have anywhere to go?"

Sam just grunted and said, "Trapped; you got Corona back there?"

The barman handed him the beer with a slice of lime stuck in the top and left him alone. Sam stared at the bar while he slowly drank his beer. He kicked himself for coming but it was too late to change things now. He tried to think of how things could have been different, but it was a futile effort. He was into his second one when someone sat on the stool next to him. He looked over and found Macy sitting there.

"I wondered if you would be here. Drowning your troubles or your memories?"

The bartender approached and asked if she wanted anything.

"I'll have what he's having."

He returned with a beer a moment later and drifted off to the other end of the bar to give them some privacy. The rest of the place was empty, so they had the bar to themselves.

"I didn't mean to make you leave," she said after a long pull from her drink.

Sam took a drink from his own bottle. He wondered if she was going to want to talk about their feelings. His feelings for her were a subject he desperately wanted to avoid, especially after a couple of beers.

"I shouldn't have come here. I thought we would talk and laugh about the old times for a while, then go our separate ways. But instead, I'm sharing a room with the—" he stopped before he finished the sentence. "But instead, I'm sitting here drinking, trying not to remember anything about the last three years."

She studied a burn mark on the bar for a while. "When I saw you tonight, I couldn't believe my eyes. You've crossed my mind every time I've flown and anytime a sail boat passes. Suddenly you were right there in front of me and I didn't know what to do."

He laughed. "I know, so many times I thought about what I wanted to say to you if I saw you again, and it all just went away the moment we were face to face."

"I've missed you. That's what I've wanted to say all night to you."

He looked at her and let out a deep breath. "There hasn't been a single day I haven't thought about you."

"So where does that leave us?" she asked.

"Damn if I know."

The bartender came back to tell them he needed to close down for the night. Sam finished his beer and paid the tab. They walked back to the room in silence and he went straight into the bathroom. When he came out, it was dark and she appeared to be asleep. He went to his bed and fell into it with a thousand thoughts racing through his tired mind.

The sound of someone moving around woke him. It took a few seconds to recall where he was and who was with him. Macy stepped out of the bathroom in her underwear before noticing he was awake.

"Sorry, I didn't realize you were awake," she said stepping back into the bathroom. She came out a moment later wearing a bathrobe. "The bathroom's all yours."

He sat on the edge of the bed and smiled weakly. "Thanks, but I think we should talk." She stopped and waited for him to start. "First off; I would like to apologize for the way I acted last night. Between the beer and the shock of seeing you after so long, I didn't know how what to do and I'm afraid I ended up screwing everything up."

"There's no need to apologize. If anything, it was my fault for assuming you still wanted me after leaving you like I did."

"You didn't assume wrong, I love you as much now as I did the day we parted. I just couldn't understand how someone I thought loved me so much, could just disappear from my life."

She sat on the foot of her bed and looked at the floor. "I should explain what happened back then," she said, wiping at her eyes. "A week before the competition, my father came to me with the chance of a lifetime. I had tried twice to get a job with the Blue Water Group, studying the effects of coral on the Costa Rican ecosystem. They had turned me down both times. Then my father shows up with an acceptance letter from them saying, I could start a week after graduation. I was so excited about the job, I couldn't wait to tell you about it; but there was a condition he was quick to tell me about. In order to get the job, he'd made a large donation to the group. In fact, the job was funded by his generosity. The condition of his donation was that I could not have any contact with you once

I started. If I did, he would stop the funding and my job would be gone, along with the trust fund he'd put aside for me. If I stayed away from you for two years, he would finance my own research vessel and hand over the trust fund for me to live off of; that was the deal I was faced with, and I'm very ashamed to say I chose it over you."

He sat beside her on the bed. "That couldn't have been an easy decision to make. I hate he put you in that position because of me."

She reached out and grabbed his hand.

"It wasn't your fault; it was my parents' fault. They wanted to get me as far away from you as they could and they knew what buttons to push to make that happen."

She could see him thinking hard, trying to accept what she told him.

"If you're wondering why Uncle Jack didn't tell you; it was because my dad lied to him and told him that I had decided to leave you. He wasn't totally convinced, but I wasn't here to tell him any different so he never contacted you."

Sam felt sick that they had been victimized by a professional bully. He had no idea that someone could be as cruel or spiteful as her father.

"I will tell you that if I ever see your father, I'll be hard pressed not to knock out a few of his teeth. I don't understand how anyone could do that to their own child."

She let him vent his anger for a moment.

"Six months ago, he finally handed over my ship and half of my inheritance. He claimed to be keeping the other half as my retirement fund. I told him that he could keep the rest and I was tired of living under his thumb. Since I had the title to the ship and enough money to fund my own research, I told him I never wanted to see him again and left Raleigh. I've been in Norfolk getting the ship outfitted since then and was traveling between there and Honduras, where I have a new project. I was on my way down there, when I ran into you."

Sam was quiet while he thought through everything. He let out a long breath.

"Despite everything that's happened, I've never stopped loving you," he said at last. "If you still want me, I'm yours."

She threw her arms around him and held him tightly. "Of course I still want you."

He kissed her deeply, like he used to. "Then it looks like we have some catching up to do," he said with a smile.

GARRY RICHARDSON

Chapter 5

He finally reached the safety of Trinidad. The storm front was still raging, but the wind slacked off considerably once he'd reached the port of Guayaguayare. He dropped anchor and made sure it was secure before heading below out of the freezing cold rain. The old man was exhausted but forced himself to slow down and secure the boat. Once he was satisfied he wouldn't sink his little home, he pulled off his rain soaked clothes and set them on the stairs to dry, then headed to his cabin and collapsed across the bed. He could hear the wind and feel the swells rocking the boat. Outside, the storm was still unleashing its fury but he'd learned long ago to sleep during the tantrums the ocean threw. He closed his eyes and she again joined him in his dreams. The old man let his tired mind send him visions of another meeting with her.

He stood on the deck of a three-mast cutter, slicing its way through the entrance to the small harbor at Roatan, Honduras.

"Drop the mainsheets and standby on the fores," he shouted as they closed slowly on the cargo dock.

Dividing his attention between the sails, the wind and the dock; he ordered the rest of the sails dropped, guiding the 130-foot cutter *Carolina* carefully to the dock. Ropes were thrown to the waiting longshoremen who were quick to secure the lines fore and aft. Sam heard cheering and turned in the direction of the sound. A large cruise ship was docked across the harbor and the cheers were from the throng of vacationers lining the rails, watching them dock. Sam laughed as he watched his first mate take a bow for the crowd.

"Mr. Stephens, please alert the Customs agent that we're ready to offload at his convenience," Sam said merrily.

The first mate nodded and headed off to follow his orders. "Aye, Sir."

"Captain, there's a message for you from the *Wayfarer*," one of the crewmen said.

Sam headed down to the radio room where the crewman on watch handed him a handwritten message.

Meet me in the city, 19:00, Emerald.

Sam smiled writing down a reply for the crewman to send.

I'll see you at our favorite place, Romeo.

He went back up to the deck and found the customs officer waiting for him. Once the man checked their cargo, he signed off on their manifest, allowing the crew to begin unloading. Sam watched the unloading operation, making sure the cargo was out of his care before relaxing.

"Mr. Stephens, I have business in town tonight. The crew has earned liberty for making us look good today. The fire watch should be sufficient until we return."

Stephens nodded and smiled along with the crew members who were close enough to hear the announcement.

"Aye, aye, sir! You heard the captain! Let's get this ship stowed or no one is going ashore tonight!"

He had some time to kill before his date so he took his time getting ready. He would have preferred for her meet him here and have the ship's cook, Smitty, fix something nice for them. But Bella's was a good second choice. He was excited to see Macy again; it had been six months since he'd last seen her. Since their reunion in Atlanta, they'd stayed in touch and rekindled the relationship they thought was lost. With nothing else to do at the time, Sam pitched in to help get her vessel ready for its research trip and spend a little time with Macy. When she left for Honduras, Sam went on vacation, sailing down to the Bahamas. During a stop in Nassau, he met an old sea captain named Chip Wheeler, who owned one of the few cargo companies still using sails to transport goods. Over drinks in a small bar, Sam and Chip talked sailing and business late into the night. The next day, Chip offered to show Sam the cutter he commanded. By evening, Sam had talked the old man into selling him the company and retiring. Sam took his sailboat back to Hilton Head and Captain Wheeler met him in Savanah, Georgia a week later. Alex told him he was crazy for getting into what looked like a losing business, but Sam ignored him. Macy was shocked when he showed up in Honduras, explaining he was not only the captain the newly-christened *Carolina*, but the owner. To the delight of the crew, she came aboard and told stories about their new captain over dinner. Since then, the two of them met whenever they were within a hundred miles of each other or their work brought them to the same ports. Her ship, the *Wayfarer*, was more modern than the *Carolina* and took less crew to operate. Sam was twenty-seven now and had enjoyed his last five years as a captain of a sailing ship. The last time Alex asked him about coming home, Sam laughed.

"Alex, I've finally found something that suits me and touches my soul. There's something special about being out there on the ocean with nothing but the wind to move you. I feel like the last pirate on the ocean, the last of a dying breed."

Alex told him he was crazy, and that he and Macy should settle down together. Sam considered it for a while but he wasn't sure how she would feel about giving up her research to be a wife. At their last meeting in Cancun, Sam mentioned settling down and she laughed.

"Is your biological clock ticking?" she asked him jokingly. He'd only shrugged at the time because he wasn't sure what she wanted.

Sam checked the time and finished getting ready. He managed to hail a cab and listened to the sounds of a reggae band failing to imitate Bob Marley while the cabbie drove the five miles into town. Sam arrived early and was greeted by Leah, the owner of Bella's. She met Sam and Macy two years ago and heard their story while they dined. She was crying by the time they finished and had become a close friend.

"You come back to Bella's to meet your true love?" Leah asked playfully. Sam grinned and hugged her. "I give you most romantic table."

Sam followed her to the second floor of the building where an open terrace looked out toward the bay. The sun was starting to turn the sky into subtle shades of reds and orange, slowly sinking over the rim of the world. Leah brought Macy in a few minutes later. Sam stood, hugged, and then kissed her, not caring if Leah was watching.

When they were done, Leah lightened the mood. "Time for kissing later; right now, wine and food."

"You look great," he told Macy once Leah was gone.

"Thank you, you don't look bad yourself. Life on a ship seems to suit you."

They caught up over a light white wine and salads. Their meal consisted of local fare lovingly prepared by Leah's husband, Ricardo. Sam noticed during dinner Macy wasn't as lively as she was at their last meeting.

"Is something bothering you?" he asked once they were alone.

She looked at him a moment before answering. "No, nothing's wrong, I've just had a lot on my mind. Actually, I've been thinking a lot about you."

"I've been thinking about you too," he said, reaching for her hand. Before he could touch her, she put her hand in her lap. Sam knew something was wrong, but waited for her to explain.

"Sam, I've been offered a new job. It's back in the States, teaching marine biology at Duke."

"That's wonderful news. Have you made a decision yet?" he asked, trying to sound happy for her, despite the knot forming behind his breastbone.

She looked into his eyes and he saw she'd already decided. Her eyes began to tear slightly and he moved to head it off.

"You'll make a great professor; just don't go around hitting on the male students."

She laughed lightly. "I promise I won't. Besides, they wouldn't be interested in an old woman like me," she said, wiping her eyes.

He reached out and she gave him her hand. "There is no woman in the world more beautiful than you."

She squeezed his hand, "I'm glad someone thinks so."

"When do you leave for home, Professor?"

She made a face at him. "I leave day after tomorrow. I'm staying in a condo south of town. I'd be happy if you would join me until I leave."

Sam put on his best smile. "It would be my pleasure."

The *Carolina* was scheduled to leave the next day, but Sam pushed back the sail date another day so they could say goodbye properly. The machine parts he was hauling to Santa Cruz del Sur, Cuba could wait a little longer. They caught a cab to his ship, and then went to her condo. She led him straight to her room where they made love like it was the last time they'd ever see each other. Sam held her in his arms while she drifted off to sleep, wondering if it really would be the last time they'd be together. He fell asleep without an answer to his question. She woke him the next morning with a kiss, which led to another round of lovemaking. Sam enjoyed their exertions, but knowing she was leaving soon, stole most of the happiness from being with her. They took a break from each other to eat breakfast and walk on the beach. They returned to the condo when the temperature reached ninety. They dined again with Leah, who cried after learning Macy was going home. When they reached the condo, Macy dragged him back to the bedroom again. Sam felt the passion in her touch and her kisses. He held her tightly, afraid she would vanish if he let her go. The whole time they made love, he looked into her eyes, trying to burn the image of her into his mind. After, Macy fell asleep, but Sam was wide awake. He lay beside her, listening to her snore lightly, while he wondered what they would do now. Sam had his fledgling business to build and Macy was going home to teach. How would they make a long-distance relationship work? Sam realized they couldn't and the reason Macy wanted him here was to say goodbye. The thought depressed him and he got up, leaving her in the bed alone. He was asleep on the couch when she found him. She tried again to get him into bed, but his heart wasn't in it. Too soon, it was time for her to head for the airport. Sam went with her all the way to the gate, to see her off. She kissed him when they announced her flight.

"Come and visit me when you can," she told him. "I'll write to you when I get settled, so you'll know where to find me."

Sam smiled past the lump in his throat. They called for boarding on her flight and it suddenly became real; they were parting again.

"Uncle Jack is meeting me at the airport and told me he has a surprise for me when I get back," she said, trying to delay saying goodbye. "Why is it that every time we get together something pulls us apart?"

He put his arms around her. "Odysseus found his way back to his love and someday I will too. I'll get up there before too long."

She began to cry softly and kissed him again. "I love you."

"I love you," he replied looking into her deep green eyes.

She had to rush to make it to the plane before they closed the doors. Sam watched the plane taxi away from the gate and let out a sigh before heading back to his boat. Within thirty minutes of his return, they were sailing out of the harbor.

Once they were away from shore, he checked the course and volunteered for the midnight watch. He went to his cabin and sat behind his desk where he allowed his tears to flow freely, wondering why this torment had been inflicted on him. His reference to Odysseus was more accurate than he'd realized. Both were sailors who wanted nothing more than a home and someone to return to. While they didn't see each other but a few times a year, it was more than he'd get to see her now. He tried to work to get his mind off of his problems, but he found he couldn't concentrate. He finally gave up and tried to get some sleep.

He awoke to the sound of a knock on his door. It was Smitty bringing his supper. Sam thanked him and ate alone, not wanting to dampen the spirits of the officer's mess. When he finished he went up on deck. His watch wasn't for a few more hours, so he went up in the rigging to be alone. He climbed to the top of the Main mast and watched the sun set from the crow's nest. While he was there, he checked the lines and yard arms to make sure of their condition and stayed in the rigging until it was time for his watch. The midnight watch was Sam's favorite. It gave him a chance to study the stars and think, while the ship was silent. With only a few lookouts and a small crew to maintain the sails, it was the quietest a ship could be, unless it was docked. Some of the crew joked, behind his back, that he was secretly a vampire and that was the reason he preferred the night watch. Sam heard them and played along, going about his duties wearing a long black cloak and his hair slicked back for a week. He stood off to the side of the wheelhouse in the dark and looked up at the stars. He reflected on his time with Macy and smiled.

At least we had a few days with each other. He smiled, remembering their last night together. He gazed at the stars, searching for answers in the constellations. A shooting star flashed across the dark sky and he made a wish. He heard the bell ring once signaling the hour. Unbidden, a thought leapt into his head, *It's a crazy world and you never know what's beyond the horizon.*

Chapter 6

The sounds of seagulls roused him and he sat up slowly. Pain in his back, arms and legs reminded him of his age and the battle he fought the night before. The boat was swaying gently on the swells, telling him the storm was past. He pushed his discomfort aside and headed for the galley to start a cup of coffee. He added two aspirin to his breakfast of fresh cut pineapple and mango. Finally, the old man adjusted his sunglasses, limping slowly up the steps to the deck. The sky was clear with only a trace of clouds trailing the cold front at a distance. The wind was blowing steady from the west, but not hard enough to be of concern. Despite being tired and sore, there was an anxiety behind his actions. Once satisfied everything was in order, he hauled in the anchor and began the process of raising the sails. He was still a long way from his destination, yet unable to shake a sense of urgency he couldn't explain. The boat began to move under him, the wind curving the sails once again. He returned to the cockpit to trim the canvas and begin navigating around the island of Trinidad. His thoughts were still on his dream of being captain of the *Carolina* and on her leaving. He felt a pain in his chest as he remembered the next time he saw her, the memory, even after all this time, stirring anger in his chest and bringing tears to his eyes. He wiped away his tears, setting his course north for the next leg of his journey. With the wind singing in the rigging and the crash of the bow in the waves, he let the memories claim his mind again.

He was off the coast of Panama, completing his transit from the Pacific to the Atlantic, when her message caught up to him. He had been at sea for a little over six months making a delivery to Valparaiso, Chile.

I need to see you immediately, please hurry,

Macy.

That was all the note said. Sam was in a panic once he read it. She had never made a request of him like this and something must have been terribly wrong, for her to make it now. He quickly changed course to the closes port and turned over command to Mr. Stephens. When they put him ashore in Colon, Sam bought a one-way ticket to Raleigh and tried to call her at home, but there was no answer. He tried to relax on the flight, but his mind was filled with every conceivable thing that could be wrong with her. His trip to Raleigh felt like it had taken a hundred years by the time he touched down. He called her cell again and this time she answered.

"Where are you?" he asked, full of concern. "Are you alright?"

"I'm at the Duke University Hospital in room 4230, I'm ok, but I need to see you."

He felt tightness in his chest. "I'm in Raleigh at the airport, I'll be there soon."

He caught a cab and was at the hospital with only thirty minutes left in visiting hours. It took him half that long to find her room. His heart pounding, he opened the door, scared of what he would find. What he saw staggered him. She was lying in the hospital bed surrounded by monitors. He noticed the bulge in her stomach and he looked at her in shock.

"Sam, we're going to have a baby."

His mind raced, trying to take in the news. He walked over to her and took her hand.

"Are you alright?" she asked.

He seemed to snap out of his shock at the question. "Yes," he said closing his eyes and whispering a silent prayer of thanks. "I thought something was wrong with you, I thought you were dying."

She put her hand on his face. "I'm sorry, I didn't mean to scare you, but I thought this was something I needed to tell you in person. I've been debating whether I should tell you or not and finally decided you should know."

He could only stare at her. She winced a little and put his hand on her stomach.

"He's a kicker."

Sam could feel a hard thump against his hand when the baby kicked.

"Wait, did you say 'he'?"

She grinned. "It's a boy, but I haven't picked out a name yet."

Sam pulled a chair over and sat beside her.

"Why didn't you tell me about this sooner?"

She looked away from him. "I didn't find out until I was back here for three months. Then I was afraid of what you might say; that you would accuse me of trying to trap you into marriage. I was so excited to finally have a piece of our love with me all of the time that I couldn't think straight. I had decided I was going to raise this child on my own and tell you when the time was right; but Aunt Lynn talked me into telling you now and giving you the chance to be here."

Sam was overwhelmed by everything he'd heard.

A nurse appeared at the door. "Sir, I'm going to have to ask you to leave. Visiting hours are over."

He looked at her and shook his head. "I'm not going anywhere until my baby arrives."

The nurse looked at Macy and she nodded that it was alright. "Well, then, we need to get you checked in, too," the nurse said with a smile.

Sam spent the night in a chair sitting next to her and his unborn child. He'd been on the midnight watch for so long he had a hard time sleeping at night. Sam also found it hard to sleep without the motion of a ship's deck beneath him, so he sat and thought about everything she'd told him. There were millions of thoughts and feelings that he had to sort through. How would he run a business that was located in the Caribbean? What kind of father would he be? Where would they live? Who would captain the *Carolina*? How soon could they get married? All of these things were running through his mind while he sat and watched his true love lying there, breathing softly. He had given up on becoming a father long ago and now, faced with the prospect, it scared him to death. He finally fell asleep with all of these questions racing around in his head. He felt like he'd barely closed his eyes when he heard the nurse come in to check on her. He watched while the nurse wrote down her vitals on a chart and quietly left. His stomach rumbled and he remembered that he hadn't eaten anything since breakfast the morning before. He walked outside the room and smelled coffee coming from the nurse's station.

"Can I help you, sir?"

"Can I buy a cup of coffee from you?"

"Help yourself."

He went behind the counter and poured some of the warm liquid into a Styrofoam cup. He added enough sugar to cut the bitterness and came back around the counter.

"Thank you."

"Do you sail?" the nurse asked him. He seemed a little confused until she pointed to the emblem on his shirt.

"Oh, yes. I'm the captain of the *Carolina*, a three-mast cutter."

"So, you're the one we were waiting for."

He gave her another confused look. "Your wife was insistent that she wait for you to get here. She scared us a few times during her pregnancy."

Sam was surprised at the news. "Has she had problems?" he asked, now concerned for both her and the baby.

"Nothing major, but she is a little past the time when most women have children. I doubt that she could have another one."

Sam sipped at his coffee for a moment. "Will it be long before the baby comes?"

"Probably not, given how far along she is."

She got a call from another room and went to check on them, leaving him there alone. He wandered back to the room and took up his position by her bed. He found himself praying that both of them would be alright.

He was still at his vigil when the sun came up and began to brighten the room. She opened her eyes and saw him sitting there watching her.

"Hello, beautiful."

She smiled at him warmly. "Hey there. Did you sleep?"

He nodded so that she wouldn't worry about him.

"How do you feel?"

"Like I have a watermelon in my stomach. I don't think it will be much longer."

"We need to discuss what we are going to do after this."

She frowned slightly. "Sam, let's take one thing at a time. I'm not worried about tomorrow, I'm worried about today."

"Ok, but when this is over, we are going to have some major decisions to make."

"I know," she replied softly.

The nurses moved them all to a delivery room when her contractions began. Jack and Lynn arrived at the start of visiting hours and were surprised to find Sam there. Lynn checked on her niece while Jack and Sam went out in the hall to catch up. They were all sitting around in the room when the door opened again and George and Sophie McCoy were standing there. Sam stood and assumed a protective stance over Macy. Macy was surprised to see them. Her father looked at Sam and then at his daughter.

"We heard you were here and wanted to make sure you were alright."

Macy reached out and held Sam's hand. "We're fine."

Sam admired the strength it took her to stand up to them. Her mother bowed her head.

"If you'll let us, we would like to be here for the birth of our grandchild," Sophia said in the silence that followed.

Macy looked up at Sam for his opinion. To the surprise of everyone he nodded yes. "It would be a shame for our child's life to start without the love of his grandparents. It's your decision, but I say let them stay." She squeezed his hand and had tears in her eyes when she smiled at him. "You can stay provided that you can be nice to Sam. If there's one word from either of you about him, I will take this child and you will never see him again. Understand?"

Her father looked like he would argue but her mother cut off whatever he might have said.

"We agree, honey."

They took turns sitting in the room with her. Jack and Lynn would move down to the waiting room, while her parents would stay and then they would swap. Sam stayed the whole time, refusing to leave her side. When the contractions started, he held her hand and tried to help as best he could. After several hours of her labor the doctor came in and made everyone leave except Sam. She checked her out and frowned.

"I'm going to take a look with an ultrasound, but I'm pretty sure that the baby is breached," She told them. "If we can't get the baby in the right position, then we'll have to do a C-section."

Macy looked scared and Sam tried to calm her. "It is going to be alright," he said softly. "We're going to be a happy little family, just try and relax."

The ultrasound showed what the doctor feared and she made a decision.

"Dad, I'm going to ask that you step outside for a while. I'll send one of the nurses out to get you when we're done."

Macy was suddenly terrified and begged to have him stay.

"Alright, he can stay but he has to scrub in," the doctor agreed, finally.

A nurse took Sam into a room where he had to wash thoroughly and put on a set of scrubs over his clothes. He returned within a few minutes and found Macy more relaxed but still scared and tense.

"I'm here," he told her, returning to her side.

"You stay up on that end and let me work on this end," the doctor told him.

He nodded and let her focus on her work. Sam told Macy about his trip into the Pacific and described the beautiful sights that he had seen there. It seemed to help her focus and relax her a bit. After a few moments, they heard the sound of a baby's cry.

"Congratulations, it's a boy."

A nurse took the baby to a side table to clean him, and then wrapped him quickly in a warm blanket before taking him to meet his proud parents. Macy held the baby for a moment, her face aglow with love and wonder. Sam watched the two of them for a second, wishing he could save this moment forever. She handed the baby over to him and he gently cradled his child in his arms for the first time. He only got to hold him for a moment before the nurse came to take him to the nursery.

"Dad, why don't you go tell everyone how perfect he is," the doctor suggested.

Sam leaned down and kissed Macy gently. He left her in the care of the doctor and three nurses and went out into the hall where he spotted Jack.

"I have a son," he said with a big smile.

Lynn followed Jack out of the room when he came down the hall to shake Sam's hand. Sam led them to the nursery and they looked through the window at the baby.

"I need to get back and check on Macy," he told them as they crowded around the window for a look. He stepped past them and started back up the hall.

"Sam" he heard Mr. McCoy say behind him. "Could I have a word?"

Sam stopped and turned around slowly. Catching a glimpse of Jack's face, he looked at the man who had caused Macy so much suffering over the last twelve years and waited to hear what he had to say.

"Sam, I know you and I have never seen eye to eye," George said slowly. "I've made things difficult for you and Macy. I deserve all of the hate you must feel towards me; but after seeing the baby and your devotion to Macy, it's made me think about a few things. If we prove this is your child, I intend to make everything right between you and my daughter,"

Sam felt the incredible urge to hit him as hard as he could; but before he could clench his fist, a surge of movement caught his eye. Sam watched Jack do what Sam had so long wanted to do. George had not seen his younger brother easing up beside him while he spoke. The punch landed with the force of a hammer and snapped George's head back sending him to the floor.

"You will leave them alone, or so help me, I will do everything in my power to ruin you," Jack declared. "George, you're my brother and I have stayed silent far longer than I should have on this. Macy and Sam have endured nothing but trouble from you since the day she brought him home. A man of lesser character would have given up on what would seem like a lost cause. But Sam has shown a love toward your daughter that amazes me. Despite every obstacle that you have put in his path, he has stayed true to her. Your blind arrogance and hatred towards him has forced your daughter to refuse to see or talk to you for the last five years."

George pulled out a handkerchief and dabbed at the blood coming from his nose and lip.

"He's nothing but a sailor, how can he afford to raise a child?" George asked him. "She will not run off and raise my grandson like some vagabond."

Jack shook his head sadly. "They can do whatever they damn well please. It's their son, not yours. In case you didn't know it, Sam makes more than you do each year. He owns his own shipping company and has amassed a small fortune. This sailor could buy everything you own and it wouldn't even dent his wallet."

George looked from Jack to Sam. "Is this true?"

"I have to get back to Macy," Sam said, leaving them and heading back up the hall. A nurse stopped him at the door.

"I'm sorry but you can't go in there right now."

"I'm the father and I would like to see her."

The woman had a sad look on her face. "You will have to wait until the doctor comes out."

Sam was suddenly worried. "What's going on? Is she alright?"

"Please wait out here and the doctor will be with you in a few minutes."

Sam felt a hand on his shoulder and turned to see Lynn standing there with Sophia.

"They won't let me in, something's wrong."

"She's tough, she'll be alright."

Sam looked at her blankly. Lynn led him to a row of chairs where they could sit down.

"I can't lose her, Lynn. She's my reason for getting up each day. I can't imagine a life without her."

Lynn put her arm around his shoulders. "Whatever happens, you have a son to consider. He's going to need his father."

"I know; I won't let him down."

"If you show him the same devotion that you have shown his mother, he'll have all he ever needs," Sophia said, surprising Sam and Lynn.

Sam looked up, hearing her voice.

"You may not think so, but I love my daughter. At first, I agreed with George and opposed you seeing Macy. When you remained faithful to her despite all we did to separate you I began to realize you truly loved her. George will possibly never see it, but I do. I don't wish to miss out on the life of my grandson; I ask your forgiveness, though I don't deserve it."

Sam sat back and closed his eyes for a moment. There were too many feelings running through him for his mind to work effectively.

"Mrs. McCoy, once I'm sure Macy's okay, we can discuss other things. Right now, she's my main concern."

Jack joined them a few minutes later. Each time someone came out of the room Sam would ask for information. The nurses refused to tell him anything, adding to his stress and concern. When his frustration level had just about reached its end; the doctor came out to talk to him.

"How is she?" Sam asked longing for good news and dreading the worst.

The woman let out a long breath. "She's stable for now. She lost a lot of blood, due to a tear in her uterus. It's taken me a while to get her patched up again. Right now, we're going to monitor her and watch for signs of a possible infection. I'll be staying until I know she's out of the woods, but I can't tell you when it will be."

For the next two days Sam alternated between the nursery and her room. He learned to change and feed his son, while the nursing staff stifled laughs at his expense. The baby still didn't have a name, because Sam wanted to make sure Macy didn't have his name picked out already. The doctor found him in the nursery rocking and gently patting his son's back, a half empty bottle beside the rocker.

"I wanted to tell you that Macy's awake, but very weak." The doctor began playing with the baby. "She's asking to see the two of you."

Sam thanked her and took off down the hall. Several nurses tried to slow him down but he ignored them. He entered the room, cradling their son against his chest and saw how weak she looked.

"Hello, beautiful," Sam said while she smiled at them. "I have someone who's been looking for you."

Sam handed her the baby and kissed her on the forehead. Tears rolled down her face when she looked at her baby.

"What did you name him?"

"I was waiting on you to help me with that one."

"I wanted to name him after my grandfather and you."

"How about both of our grandfathers?"

"Jason was what I wanted to name him."

"I like it. Thomas was my grandfather's name."

"Then he will be Jason Thomas Richards."

A nurse appeared at the door and within a few minutes the birth certificate was filled out. Sam took the baby to feed him while she visited with her family. She was shocked when Sam asked her mother if she wanted to hold Jason. Once they left them alone, Macy gave him a questioning look

"What was the deal with you and mom?"

Sam smiled. "We're trying a cease fire, but it doesn't include your father."

She looked sad at the news. He explained what happened between her father and Jack. She let out a sigh.

"At least you behaved," she said, giving him a tired smile.

"You should get some rest."

"Are you going to start telling me what to do now?"

"Just until you are able to get up and move around again."

A bassinet was brought in and Sam put Jason in it to sleep for a while. Macy was sleeping and he sat back, closing his tired eyes for a moment.

The sound of Macy calling his name woke him in what felt like only seconds later. He looked around to get his bearings and heard Jason crying in the bassinet and Macy laughing at him.

"I think your son is looking for you," she said while he rubbed his face.

He got up and picked up the child and then handed the baby to her while he went in search of a bottle. The crying stopped as soon as she held him. Sam went down to the nursery and started making a bottle. The nurse on duty grinned as she watched him finish and start back up the hall. "You're going to be a good daddy."

He just laughed in reply and went back to the room. He handed over the bottle and Macy fed her baby for the first time.

It took three days for her to recover enough to be moved to a regular room. Once there, Sam and Macy were visited by a long line of her students. Many of them were already volunteering to take on some of the babysitting duties. It was the first time that Sam had seen Macy's effect on her students. Macy greeted each of them by name and it was clear to Sam that she took the time to get to know all of her students. Her parents stopped by for a brief visit and for the first time ever her father was actually polite to Sam. Sam wondered how much of it was due to Sophia's influence and how much of it was due to Jack's revelation about him. Sam tried not to think about it too much and focused instead on making sure Macy was healing. The doctor made an appearance and finally announced that both mother and son were fit to go home.

Jack drove the family to the house Macy owned near the university. It was a nice ranch style house, a few minutes away from the campus. Her students had decorated the yard in blue and several were waiting for them when they arrived. She had been in the hospital for a week and was ready to be home.

After the welcoming committee left, Sam and Macy were finally alone again with their son. Sam rocked him to sleep while Macy went through a long list of emails on her computer. He put Jason in his crib and got two bottles ready before joining her on the couch.

"We need to talk now that everything's settling down."

She sighed and put her head on his shoulder.

"I know."

"Do you want a simple ceremony or something big?"

"What?"

"For our wedding; I want you to marry me."

She shook her head. "Why?"

He was confused. "What do you mean, why? We have a child to raise and take care of. We can finally be together and be a family."

She looked down at the cushion on the couch.

"Sam, I don't want to get married," she said at last. He felt his heart stop beating for a second.

"I love you and I want you to be a part of Jason's life. But we've never spent a lot of time together. One of us has constantly been on the move since we met. What if we're suddenly together all the time and we couldn't stand each other? I would rather stay like we are, than lose you."

Sam was silent for a long time. She sat up and looked at him.

"Say something."

"When you were in the room and the doctor was fighting to save you, I couldn't help but regret all the time that we've been apart. I've wanted to stand by your side and sleep next to you for as long as I can remember. To hear you say that you don't want to marry me hurts."

She put her hand on his cheek. "I'm so sorry to hurt you, and I'm not saying that I don't want you in my life or in my bed. You're the only man I have ever been with and the only one that I'll ever love. We don't need a piece of paper to tell us how much we mean to each other, do we?"

He shook his head slowly. "So, what do we do now?"

"First, we go to bed. It's been too long since I've woke up next to you. We'll work out the rest later."

He nodded slowly, getting up and heading for her room. He didn't like her plan but kept his mouth shut for now. She stopped and checked on the baby on the way to her room. Sam stood at the door and watched her fuss over him. They finally retired for the night, but Sam found he couldn't sleep. There were too many things on his mind. He went back to check on his son and found him awake. Sam picked him up and took him in the den where he fed him again. A few minutes of rocking had him back to sleep, and Sam laid him back down in his crib. He couldn't get the conversation with Macy out of his head. He wanted them to be a family, but she seemed determined to raise their son on her own. He was still thinking things though when he drifted off to sleep, sitting on the couch. He woke up at daylight and heard Macy moving around in the back of the house somewhere. He got up and found her dressing Jason on the floor of the nursery.

"You weren't there when I woke up this morning," She said once she noticed him. "I found you asleep on the couch. Did you get up with him last night?"

"I fed him a little after midnight and rocked him back to sleep. I couldn't sleep so I went to think some things through and fell asleep out there."

She finished dressing the baby and looked over at Sam while she played with him.

"What were you thinking so hard about?" she asked, already knowing what it was.

"I still don't understand why you won't marry me," he said finally. "I can take care of you and Jason. You could work if you wanted to or stay home with him. I can run the shipping company from anywhere; work isn't a problem. I don't want to be an absent father. I want to go to baseball games and see his first steps."

"Sam we've been through this," she said. "We're too set in our ways to try and adjust to each other's lives. It's going to be hard enough to adjust to a baby. This was exactly why I didn't want to tell you about him; because I knew how you would react. You're an old-fashioned guy and it makes you easy to predict."

"So, I'm a bad guy because I think our son should have both his parents?"

"I'm not saying you're a bad guy. You just don't get the fact that I don't want to change you. God, most men would be thrilled to get a deal like this."

"I'm not most men," he said leaving, her in the room with Jason, who began to cry.

Sam felt frustrated at her resistance. Over the next week he tried to understand but he couldn't rectify her love for him with her refusal to accept his proposal. He finally began sleeping on the couch instead of sharing her room, adding more tension between them. Jason sensed the turmoil and was fussy, keeping them awake all night. Sam was worn out; after his second night being up with Jason and Macy's stubbornness over marriage, he moved his things out of her room.

"Why haven't you been sleeping in the room with me?" she asked him after finding his clothes gone.

"Because I won't sleep beside you knowing you don't want me to stay."

She refused to talk to him the rest of the day and went to bed without even saying goodnight, leaving him to deal with Jason again while she slept.

Sam began to feel like she was ready for him to leave. Jack came by to visit and while Lynn and Macy were playing with Jason, he took Jack outside to talk about what was going on.

"Jack, I don't know what else to do," Sam said in frustration. "I've asked her a dozen times to marry me, but she refuses. I don't want to be a drop-in father, but what other choice do I have?"

Jack was silent while he thought. "I don't know what to tell you. Usually, it's the other way around, but nothing about the relationship you two have is normal."

"Jack, I'm almost to the point where I'm ready to go. I never thought I'd say that, or want to be away from Macy. Maybe she's right and this is a bad idea."

Jack put his hand on Sam's shoulder. "She's probably still got some crazy hormones left over from the pregnancy, so don't give up hope yet."

Over the next few days Macy became even more distant from him, even refusing to let him help her with Jason and still not speaking to him. Sam finally had enough and confronted her.

"I've had it with you ignoring me," he told her after she put the baby down to sleep. "If you want me gone so badly, then just say so."

"You're the one that's refusing to share my bed. All I wanted was for us to continue like we always have, but you're dead set on getting married and being a family. This is exactly what I was afraid of and look at how it turned out."

He took a deep breath to stay calm and keep from waking Jason. "So, all you want is for me to drop by when I'm around and check up on you? You just want me to warm your bed when I'm here, then leave before you have to decide how you feel? What about Jason? How's he going to feel about having a dad who's never around? He's never going to be comfortable around me, because he'll never get to know me."

Macy grunted, "Is that what you are worried about; him knowing his father?"

"That's part of it. The other part is I've loved you for most of my life and I had the crazy thought you loved me, too. I wanted to share a life with you, not just a bed."

She wouldn't look at him anymore. "Well, that isn't going to happen. If you can't accept that I love you and this is how I want things, then maybe you should leave."

Sam hung his head and stared at the floor. "Fine," he said softly, but she wasn't there to hear it. He heard the door to her room slam in the back of the house. He went into the kitchen and wrote down his phone number.

If there's ever anything Jason needs, just call, he wrote across the top.

He went back into the nursery and placed a second note on the dresser next to his son.

> *I know you will never understand, but I love you and your mother more than my own life. I want nothing more than to watch you grow into the man you'll become, but life sometimes has other plans. I hope one day you'll be able to forgive me for not being around. The choice to leave wasn't mine and however much I want to take you with me, life at sea is no way to raise a baby. If you never want to speak to me, I'll understand, though you'll be in my thoughts and prayers every day, until my last breath.*

Love always,

Dad

Sam went back through the den and picked up his sea bag. In top, he placed a small picture of Macy holding Jason. He made sure the door was locked behind him when he left. With tears streaming down his face, he couldn't imagine his heart hurting any worse.

Chapter 7

The old man checked his heading again and made a small correction. The weather had settled, though the wind was a touch colder than before the cold front passed. He checked his position on the GPS and found he had around 300 miles to go until his next rest stop. He was in the Grenada Basin, twenty miles off the coast of Dominica. At his best estimate, he was about twelve hours away from his next stop, St. Thomas. He considered stopping off in Martinique, but talked himself out of it. Of all the islands he had visited around the world, Martinique was his favorite. He'd considered buying a house and retiring there once, but she had kept him from following through on the idea. It was dusk and before him, there was a scattering of stars winking though the darkening sky. He kept a sharp eye out for traffic cutting across his path. He adjusted the trim of his sails again while the specter of his past returned. He'd been haunted by his past a lot on this trip and he wished for the first time he'd stayed in Rio.

He was thirty-three years old and though his hair was starting to turn gray, his mind and body were those of a young man. He joked that all of the salt he'd soaked in over the years had preserved him like salted pork. A few of the cargo handlers he dealt with overheard him talking about it and began calling him "Old Salt", which Sam adopted, wearing it like a badge of honor. He was in Key West to see his son, after five long years. Sam made it a habit to send Macy money to use on Jason. She was still teaching at the university, and though she didn't need the money, he sent it anyway, trying in some small way to support his child the only way she'd let him. She mailed him pictures and sometimes videos of different events in Jason's life. Sam spent hours watching each of them and soaking up every detail. His favorite picture was of Jason dressed like a pirate for Halloween the prior year. The letter with it explained that Jason was in love with ships and pirates. Sam couldn't help but smile at the idea of Jason inheriting some of the salt water flowing through his veins.

The *Carolina* was tied at a large dock in A&B Marina and the crew was given liberty to enjoy the sights of Key West. Doug Stephens, Sam's First Mate, stayed to give a few public tours to those who wanted to walk through the old sailing ship.

Sam headed for the place he would meet the two loves of his life. He was early for their lunch meeting at Bogie's. The place was decorated like a movie set, with pictures of Humphrey Bogart and scenes from his movies everywhere. It was one of Sam's favorite places in Key West and he wanted to share it with the two people he loved the most. He was shown to a table where he anxiously watched the door while he waited. He spotted Macy when she walked in with Jason beside her. He waved and caught her attention, watching her lead Jason to the table. Time had been better to Macy than it had been to him. Her hair was still black as midnight at sea and her emerald eyes still drew the attention of everyone who saw her. She moved with the grace of a dancer, though her skin wasn't tanned like it once was. He got up and gave her a hug when she reached the table. He went to kiss her and she turned her cheek to him before he could touch her lips. A second of confusion crossed his face before they parted and Sam turned his attention to the boy beside her.

"Hey there, Jason."

"Hi," he replied shyly.

"Jason, this is my friend, Captain Sam,"

Sam thought it was curious she didn't introduce him as Jason's father but he didn't say anything. They sat down as a waiter came to take their order, and then left them alone.

"Jason, I understand you like pirates?" Sam asked once the waiter moved away. The boy's eyes brightened.

"I do, Captain Hook is my favorite!"

Sam smiled at him. "Did you know I have a boat that looks like a pirate ship?"

The boy looked at him in awe. "Really? Can I see it?"

"You sure can," There was a look from Macy and Sam quickly added. "As long as your mom says it's okay."

Jason looked at his mother and begged. "Can I, please, Mom?"

She smiled at him indulgently. "We'll have to see."

Jason looked at Sam again. "Can Shaun come too?"

Sam looked at Macy for an explanation. "I don't think Shaun would like to see it," she told Jason, avoiding Sam's gaze.

"Yes, he would, he told me he liked ships and pirates, too."

"We'll ask him later," Macy said firmly, ending the conversation. She glanced at Sam, who was still watching her closely, hoping for some clarification.

"Is your pirate ship big?" Jason asked before Sam could question her about Shaun.

Sam focused on the boy. "It is a hundred and thirty feet long and has sails that make it move just like the old ships. Have you ever been sailing?"

Jason nodded. "Once, mom took me on her boat, but it sank and we can't go anymore."

"It was still tied up when a hurricane came through," she explained. "I couldn't get there to get it moved and the storm destroyed it."

Sam looked a little sad at the news. "Did the house survive?"

She shook her head slowly. "It's being rebuilt, but it'll be a while."

Their food arrived and they started eating. Sam noticed the ring when Macy reached for her glass to take a drink. He froze, seeing the diamond and what it represented. His fork fell from his hand, bouncing off the plate and falling to the floor. He felt his temper rising while his mind put all the pieces which had puzzled him, together to complete the picture. Sam wanted to scream at her, at the injustice of what she was doing to him, but then Jason caught his attention. He took a deep breath forcing the lid closed on his anger toward her. Macy saw his conflicting emotions and set her glass on the table, moving her hand out of sight, hoping he wouldn't make a scene.

"It looks like you have some exciting news to tell me about," Sam said, the calmness of his voice laced with sarcasm.

Macy slowly raised her eyes to meet his, begging him to let her explain later, in a more private setting. "Can we talk about this later and not in front of Jason?" she pleaded.

"Why not discuss it now? Aren't you proud of your engagement? We should have drinks to celebrate!" he exclaimed, his voice raising a little, drawing attention from the tables around them.

She gave him a withering glare, but he ignored it, wanting to hurt her the way she hurt him.

"Sam, you don't understand."

Sam laughed at her, he understood perfectly. He noticed the tears forming at the corners of her eyes and for a second felt sorry for her. Mentally kicking the emotion aside, his anger returned. Sam pushed his chair back and threw the napkin on his plate.

"Bring Jason and whoever else happens to be traveling with you down to the A & B Marina if they would like a tour of the ship. I would make it soon though, because it's leaving and it won't be back for a long time, if ever."

He looked at his son and wished he could hold him again. "I hope to see you soon, Jason," Sam said, tossing a fifty-dollar bill on the table to cover their lunch. "You're always welcome on the *Carolina*. I have to leave to go and check on it, okay?"

"Okay, Captain Sam," he said.

Sam didn't even look at Macy when he stormed out the door. He was angry with her and his fury only built the further down Duval Street he went. By the time he reached the ship he was in a foul temper and ready to set sail immediately. Mr. Stephens noticed the change, watching his captain stomp across the gangplank.

"Problem, Captain?" he asked gently. Sam shot him a look that would have frozen water.

Sam growled. "I'll be in my cabin and I'm not to be disturbed. The tours are closed for the day, understood?"

"Aye, Sir."

Mr. Stephens moved away quickly to avoid Sam's wrath. Sam slammed the door to his cabin and found the bottle of rum he kept in his desk drawer. He pulled out the stopper and took a long drink straight from the bottle. The liquor was bitter and burned its way down his throat. Sam slammed the bottle on the desk with a loud thump, wanting to punch something, but knowing it wouldn't help. He'd followed Jack's advice and hadn't pressured her about getting married. To ease the pain of missing out on his son's life he'd thrown himself into running the business, adding two more ships to his small fleet. The *Florida* and the *Georgia* were on their maiden voyages making deliveries to Jamaica and Barbados. Now that the business was thriving, Sam thought about settling down, perhaps building a house on the island of Martinique, then asking Macy and Jason to join him. He saw now his plans for a future with them was ruined, and worse, his heart was shattered again. The woman who had said no to him, said yes to another man. The anger built inside him until he slammed the desk top with his fist.

"Damn her!" he shouted, pounding his fist on the desk a second time.

There was a knock on the door. "Captain, I know you said you didn't want to be disturbed, but Miss McCoy is on deck asking for you," Mr. Stephens said.

"Let her stay there or kick her off my ship, your choice," he growled before he thought about Jason. "Wait; is there a boy with her?"

"Yes, sir."

Sam may be angry with Macy, but it had nothing to do with Jason. If he was here to see the ship, then he'd get a personal tour with the captain. Sam put the cork back in the bottle.

"I'll be out in a moment."

Sam went into the head and used some mouthwash to remove the smell of the rum. He straightened his clothes and went out to face them.

Jason was standing at the end of the gangplank looking wide-eyed at the ship. Behind him stood Macy, a man and a girl close to Jason's age.

"Ahoy, Jason," Sam said as he walked out onto the deck. Jason looked at him and grinned.

"Hello, Captain," he replied. Macy and the others trailed behind the boy while he raced up the gangplank.

Sam already knew who the others were and evidently the man knew about Sam. The man put his arm around Macy's waist and gave Sam a protective glare.

"Nice boat," he said, taking a jab at Sam.

"It's not a boat, it's a three-mast cutter, making her a ship," Sam corrected. "I'm Sam Richards, Captain of the *Carolina*."

The man stuck out his hand. "Captain, I am Shaun Harrison and this is my daughter Sara."

"Welcome aboard the *Carolina*," Sam said with more cheerfulness than he felt. "Come along and I'll give you the tour."

"We don't want to take up any more of your time," Macy said, wondering at his change of mood from the restaurant. "Jason just wanted to see the ship."

"Then he needs a tour and nobody knows this ship better than the captain."

He took them to the wheelhouse where they took turns moving the big wheel. Harrison produced a camera and began to take pictures of the kids. Sam offered to take a picture of all of them together at the wheel. He snapped a picture of them, realizing he'd let Shaun take his family from him without a fight. Back outside, he found a couple of the crew members who worked up in the sails. Sam excused himself and spoke to them for a moment. When he returned, they scrambled into the rigging and onto the ratlines of the mainsail.

"Jason, would you like to give the crew some orders?" he asked the boy.

Jason's eyes lit up and he nodded. "Then tell those scurvy crewmen of mine to make ready the mainsail," he said in his best pirate voice.

Jason laughed and looked up into the rigging. "Ahoy up there!" he yelled as loud as he could. "Ready the mainsail, you scurvy dogs!"

Sam had to hide a laugh while his crew went to work. The sail dropped while on the deck, several more crewmen, tied off the sail so it would catch the wind. Sam patted the boy on the shoulder.

"That was good, son; if I ever need a new first mate, I know who to call."

Jason beamed at him. Sara called out the orders to reef the sails and the crew showed off their skills, securing the canvas to the delight of the kids. He took them below and showed them where the crew ate and slept while they were off duty. Sam could see that First Mate Doug Stephens had been ahead of him and making sure everything was squared away. They finally reached his cabin.

"This is where the captain stays," he said opening the door letting them follow him inside.

The two adults stepped inside the door and the kids followed Sam around to his desk. Stephens had beaten them to the room and had placed a pair of eye patches and paper hats on Sam's desk, something they did for all the kids who came aboard on tours. Sam made a show out of giving them the patches and hats, announcing they were honorary crew members of the *Carolina*.

"Hey, that's a picture of me!" Jason said, his sharp eyes finding the picture on Sam's desk. "Mom, he has a picture of me! Maybe he can give it to my dad if he sees him?"

Sam looked at Macy with questioning eyes. "I'm sure he'll give it to him, if he runs into him." She said avoiding Sam's gaze.

"Will you, Captain Sam?" Jason asked him. Sam swallowed past the lump in his throat, ignoring Macy's betrayal to give his son hope.

"Aye, I will, lad," Sam answered. "What name does he go by?"

Jason gave him a long look. "Sam McCoy; hey, he has the same name as you!" the boy pointed out.

Sam struggled to suppress the anger building inside him again.

"I saw him not long ago, in Brazil. He was telling everyone coming this way he had a message to give you, if they ran into ya. He told them to let ya know how much he misses ya and that he loves ya dearly."

Jason looked at him for a moment and then hugged him. "Thanks, Captain Sam!" he said. Sam treasured the hug, wishing it would last longer.

Doug Stephens appeared at the door in time to hear their conversation.

"The captain has a ship to run, I'll be taking everyone back on deck now," Mr. Stephens said quickly.

Macy and Shaun herded the two kids out of the cabin and said goodbye. Macy hesitated at the door and looked back at Sam. He spun the chair around toward the porthole behind his desk without a word. Hearing the door close behind him signaled the end of everything he ever wanted. Emotionally he was drained; there was no anger now, just sadness, making his heart ache yet again. Tears streamed down his face, realizing his own son didn't even know him and the woman he loved betrayed him. There was a knock at his door a little while later.

"Captain, are you alright?" Doug asked through the door. Sam wiped at his eyes and continued to stare out of the open porthole. Behind him the door creaked open.

"Captain?" Doug asked as he stepped inside. Sam didn't turn toward him. "Sorry to bother you, Captain, but I heard what you told your boy. Why didn't you tell him the truth?"

Sam let out a deep breath. "It wouldn't have done any good. He wouldn't believe me over his mother."

Doug poured Sam a large snifter of peach brandy. "I think you could use this, sir." Sam took it and sipped at it slowly.

"Thank you, Doug, and thank you for taking care of the hundreds of details to make his trip here special. There are a lot of things I value in my life and your friendship is one of them."

"Someone has to take care of the captain."

Sam grunted, and then heard Doug move toward the door. "Mr. Stephens, please alert the crew that we will be leaving when our cargo is loaded and provisions are accounted for."

"Aye, sir."

"It's time to put this miserable island off the stern," Sam muttered to himself.

It was almost ten that evening when there was a knock on his cabin door. He was lying in his hammock wishing he could fall asleep and thinking about what to do with his life.

"Come," he said without getting up. He looked at the door when it opened and Macy came in. "How did you get onboard? Was there something you forgot to tell me while breaking my heart?"

She was stung by his words and the petty side of him felt better seeing her in pain.

"Doug let me onboard, though he was reluctant to do so. It appears I should have headed his advice and left you alone."

Sam wouldn't look at her and stared at the ceiling.

"Say what you came to say then leave. I've had enough of you today."

She was quiet for a moment. "I should have expected anger from you. I only wanted a chance to explain everything." His silence prompted her to continue. "I know today has brought you nothing but pain, and for that, I'm truly sorry. It was never my intention to hurt you."

He rolled out of the hammock and planted his feet firmly on the deck with a thump.

"You're marrying another man and my own son doesn't even know his father," he said darkly. "It sounds like your intentions are pretty clear to me."

She took a deep breath and let it out slowly. "What do you tell a four-year-old who asks where his daddy is? What does he tell his friends, who wonder why his father never comes to anything? I had to tell him something, so I made something up he could believe and was partially true to satisfy him. I fully intend to tell him the whole truth in a few years."

"I would've been there if you'd let me. You were perfectly clear you didn't need me to help raise our child, so I respected your wishes and left you alone until you decided you needed me again. Now I've lost you and my son!"

She shook her head. "You don't understand. I didn't plan this with Shaun. It just kind of happened. I was fine on my own with Jason, then I met him and his daughter Sara. His wife died of cancer and he was good with Jason. He was looking for someone to help him raise a little girl and I realized Jason needed a man around. I couldn't just call you and say, 'Sorry, I changed my mind.' So, when he asked me to marry him I said yes."

"Get off my ship. If Jason wants to stay in touch with me, I will stay in touch with him. Otherwise, I don't want anything else to do with you. I have lied to him the only time I'll ever lie to him, to give you a chance to set things right. I hope one day you'll give him the letter I left for him and he'll understand none of this was my doing."

She was crying now, her mascara leaving black trails down her face. "I'm sorry."

He walked to the porthole again and looked out across the dark water. "Goodbye, Macy."

He held his pose until he heard the door shut behind him. Once he was alone, he slumped against the wall, his hands shaking in anger and disappointment. Doug knocked a few minutes later.

"Captain, the crew is onboard and we can sail at first light with the outgoing tide."

"Very well, Mr. Stephens, I'll see to the night watch while you sleep."

"Do we have a destination, Captain?"

"Anywhere but here."

The tide turned an hour after the first rays of light came over the horizon. Under his orders the crew cut the ship loose from the dock and made sail out of the harbor without fanfare. Sam looked back once when they left the island. He thought for a moment about the excited little boy he was leaving behind and loved so much.

Forgive me again, son, he thought, watching the island getting smaller in the distance.

Chapter 8

The old man watched the sun slip below the horizon over his shoulder. He was getting into an area where there was an increase in traffic, so he decided to find a place to drop anchor for the night and get some sleep. There was a nice natural harbor on the east side of Saba Island and he steered toward it. It was fully dark by the time he reached the spot he was looking for and he was tired. He dropped the anchor and made dinner in the galley before sitting down and turning on the radio. He scanned through the dial, past stations playing music from the Mainland, until he found a local station that was playing soft Latin music. He'd developed a taste for the music while living in Rio and found it a fine traveling companion when he was alone. He ate and listened for a while before returning to the deck to gaze up at the stars, as was his practice over the many years at sea. The music from below was sad and mournful, reminding him of his past. He sat thinking about his life and how much of it had been shaped by sadness. Everything he'd wanted as a young man had slipped past him like an island breeze.

Now I'm on another fool's errand, he thought, looking up at the constellations.

Unbidden, the scenes of his son's graduation from high school and later from college brought smiles to his face. *Not everything has been bad*, he admitted grudgingly. *I've seen a lot of places and met a lot of very interesting people though the years; not to mention all the planes I've flown and the ships I've sailed. It's been interesting and unlike any other life I've heard of. This old salt has sailed nearly every ocean in the world and is still here to talk about it; though I've had some rough times, it has only made the good times more meaningful.*

He went below and crawled into his bed. Surprisingly, he didn't dream of his past. He woke up early, noticing that it was still dark outside. The galley clock showed it to be just before sunrise. He changed his clothes before going up to watch the sun peek over the horizon and to start another day. He was roughly six hours away from his next destination, Charlotte Amalie, in the Virgin Islands. He went about his normal routine of checking the boat, before pulling the anchors. Satisfied that everything was in order, he freed the boat and let it float with the outgoing tide. He floated out of the cove and raised the sails, thinking about the last time he'd been to North Carolina.

He sat in the back of the huge cathedral watching the bride walk down the aisle, escorted by her father. The white gown she wore had the air of a traditional dress while still holding to the latest styles. When the bride reached the altar, everyone was seated and Sam could see the groom in his black tuxedo. Neither the bride nor the groom would notice him, where he was sitting. He had consciously picked a spot well away from everyone, sitting by himself in the balcony, which was occupied by one member of the small army of photographers and their video equipment. During the ceremony, he noticed the couple had skipped the part asking if there were any objections to the union. His sadness grew when they made their vows to each other and slipped on their rings. The priest said a final prayer blessing the couple and their lives together, then pronounced them husband and wife. There was applause as the couple shared their first kiss under the same last name. While the music played, the happy couple walked out of the cathedral together, holding hands and smiling. Sam took a moment to look around the huge church. It had been a long time since he'd sat in a church pew. His own church was much different from the one he found himself in now. Instead of walls and pews, his church was the open sea surrounding him, with a choir of seagulls singing overhead. His organ was the sound of the wind in the sails and the shanty songs his crew sang while working. The sunlight through the stained-glass windows sent multi-colored light dancing across the crowd below, reminding him of the sun on the clear shallow water illuminating the coral and creatures of the sea. The man packing his video equipment disrupted his thoughts.

"Are you coming to the reception? I hear it'll be a great party."

He and Sam had talked before the start of the ceremony and when the man found he was a ship captain, he talked Sam's ear off.

"Perhaps I'll see you there," Sam told him. The man smiled and finished packing his gear. Sam noticed the crowd had thinned quite a bit. He found the stairs leading back to the ground floor and joined the end of the line waiting to congratulate the happy couple. He was dressed in a white suit with a light blue shirt and white tie. He hung back until he was the last person in line. The groom suddenly noticed him and rushed over. Sam thought about all the things he wanted to say, but they vanished when the groom smiled.

"Congratulations, Jason," Sam told his son, tears of pride welling in his eyes.

Jason grinned broadly. "Thanks, Dad. I didn't think you'd make it."

"Are you kidding? I wouldn't have missed this for anything."

The groom's young radiant bride joined them and Jason introduced her. "Dad, I would like you to meet Angela. Angela, this is my dad, Captain Sam Richards."

The young woman smiled warmly. "It's nice to finally meet you."

"You are a lovely bride, my dear. It's obvious Jason has impeccable taste," he said, lightly kissing her hand.

"I've been telling him that since we met."

"Dad, how long will you be here?"

"I'll be here until you two have left for your honeymoon. Then I'm heading back to sea. Which reminds me, I have something for the two of you," he said, removing an envelope from an inside jacket pocket and handing it to Jason.

Jason opened it and took out a check and a piece of paper. Jason grinned as he read the paper and handed it to his new wife.

"Are you serious?" Jason asked.

"I hope you enjoy it; you can redeem it at any time, now or later. The *Tennessee* was built as an alternative to a traditional cruise and there's a suite at your disposal whenever you want it."

Jason had handed Angela the check without looking at it along with the letter. When she gasped, he looked to see what was wrong with her and found that she was staring at the check in shock. He looked over her shoulder, then back at his dad.

"This is too much, Dad," Jason said, looking at the check.

"Son, I want you and Angela to have a better start than I did. Consider it my investment in your happiness. All I ask in return is that you bring my grandchildren to visit me sometime. Not that I'm rushing you."

Angela hugged him and thanked him for everything. Jason joined her in thanking him as well.

"I expect that there is a rather large group of people waiting for your arrival; it would be a shame for me to make you late for your reception."

They insisted he ride with them to the reception, since he would have to call a cab to take him there. Sam hadn't owned a car since he first set sail twenty-five years earlier. He shook his head realizing he'd spent nearly half of his fifty-two years with a deck under his feet. *Maybe that's why I feel so strange on land and comfortable at sea.*

They finally talked him into riding with them and he listened to the story of how they met on the drive out to the reception. During the drive, they told the story of their courtship and Jason's proposal.

The long black limousine parked in front of a house that Sam knew too well. The McCoy family home had been redecorated for the reception and Sam could see Macy's touch on the decorations. He remained in the car while the happy couple made their way through the crowd and onto the wide front porch. Sam slipped out of the opposite side once they were inside. It had been a long time since he had first seen the house. Frowning, he remembered how long it had been and how uncomfortable they made him feel. *If I had taken George's hint and left her alone, I wonder how different things would have been.*

There was a man collecting invitations at the door and for a moment Sam thought he'd have trouble getting in. A familiar voice came from the lawn behind him.

"I wondered if you would show," Jack McCoy said, approaching the door using a walker. "My brother owes me fifty bucks, thanks to you."

Sam smiled at the man and waited for him to catch up to where he was standing. "Jack, how are you?" Sam asked, glad to see a friendly face.

"I'm old and everything hurts. Come on, Lynn's waiting for me inside. I'll get you past the Gestapo." Once they were inside, Jack shook his head sadly. "One of my brother's ideas, 'got to keep out the party crashers', is how he explained it. I think the cheap bastard was trying to keep you out and win the bet."

"How is the old SOB?"

Jack stopped and looked Sam in the eye.

"The McCoy fortune is going away fast. George tied a lot of money up in land development and when the economy slowed, he lost more than he could recover. He has enough to get by, but he insists on trying to live like he used to and it's almost gone."

Sam tried not to take a little satisfaction over George's misfortune.

"How are the Harrisons?"

Jack cut his eyes at Sam. "They're fine, though they have a strange relationship."

"Really, how so?"

"She lives at the university and he lives out at the beach house, which I gave to her when she moved back here. If you're looking for her, she's over there," Jack said, pointing toward a group of women who had Angela surrounded. Sam spoke to Lynn before turning back to find Macy again.

Sam spotted Macy through the crowd and couldn't help but smile. She was still the dark-haired beauty she'd always been. He noticed a few wrinkles around her eyes, but otherwise, she hadn't changed. She wore a light pink dress that fit her slim figure nicely. She was talking to a small circle of women and didn't notice him. He hadn't spoken to her since he threw her off his ship so many years before. Standing there watching her, he realized how bad he'd treated her. He'd thought about it often during his travels and had finally forgiven her, after Jason contacted him the first time. Jason spent the summer of his fifteenth birthday aboard the *Georgia,* learning how to sail and getting to know his father. For the next three years, Jason returned and worked with Sam during the summer. Jason surprised everyone when he decided to become a Business major at Coastal Carolina, instead of Duke. Sam had seen Macy twice since Key West; at Jason's graduation from high school and again when he graduated college. Sam kept his distance and even though there was peace between them he'd still refused to talk to her.

"Well, son of a bitch, I guess I owe my brother fifty dollars," said a voice from behind him.

He turned and looked George McCoy in the face. George had aged and looked terrible. He was dressed in a suit and held a cocktail in his hand. The wheelchair he was restricted to was being pushed by a young lady Sam didn't recognize.

"George," Sam said simply.

The man looked at him for a moment and laughed. "You're like a head cold, every time I think I've gotten rid of you, you come back," George said before he started a coughing fit.

"Grandpa!" the young woman exclaimed. "You behave, this is a guest."

Sam laughed a little; he didn't know who she was, but he liked her already.

"He's no guest, he's a pest and the one who ruined my relationship with my daughter," George said grumpily.

The young woman looked at Sam for a moment. "Captain Sam?"

Sam nodded slowly.

She grinned. "I am Sara Harrison, you probably don't remember me, but I was on your ship once."

Sam smiled, remembering her and the reason she was on his ship. "Actually, I do remember, you visited with Jason a long time ago. Forgive me for not recognizing you earlier."

"So, you've gotten to another one of my girls?" George asked.

Sam looked down at the old man and felt pity for him.

"George, I hope you live to be a hundred."

George looked at him harshly. "I should have you thrown out."

Sara gave Sam a pained look. "I'm sorry for his behavior; he's usually much nicer than this."

Sam smiled warmly at her. "It's alright; George and I have an understanding. We simply agree to dislike each other, a lot."

She started to push her grandfather away and paused for a moment. "I hope we get a chance to talk again later."

Sam nodded and watched her go with a smile. He was caught by Angela and her parents, whom he liked immediately. He found the bar and was about to order when a familiar voice spoke behind him.

"He wants rum with pineapple juice on ice," Macy said.

"She'll have a lime margarita." Sam turned slowly to face her. "Hello, Macy."

"You remembered my favorite after all these years," she said. "God, I haven't had one in so long, I've forgotten what they taste like."

"Was it at Bella's before you left to come back?"

She searched for a trace of anger on his face but didn't see it. "I guess it was. Do you still eat there when you're in Honduras?"

Sam's face clouded over a moment. "No, Bella's was destroyed by a hurricane. The family decided to not rebuild."

"You look well," Macy said, changing the subject.

"You never could lie," he said, drawing a smile from her. "I look like the old man I have become. You, however, haven't aged a day in twenty years. You look fabulous."

"Still the charmer. It's amazing what a great hair dresser can do to fool people."

Sam took their drinks, handing her the Margarita. "To old times and faraway places."

She touched her glass to his and sipped her drink. "I forgot how good these are."

"Macy, is there somewhere we could talk for a few minutes?"

Sam followed her into a small library with a large bay window facing the front lawn. He closed the door behind him and waited for her to face him.

"Macy, I owe you an apology, I lashed out at you in Key West because I was hurt. I wish I could have that moment back so I could change it, but all I can do is beg your forgiveness."

She closed her eyes and exhaled a deep breath. "Sam, I forgave you long ago," she said, opening her eyes to look at him. "Shaun and I only lived together for a year before he moved to the beach and left me with both kids. Instead of getting help with Jason, I suddenly found myself with two kids and a husband who only wanted to hang out on the beach or throw money at the stock market. I wanted to write and tell you how wrong I was, explain how much I missed you, but you had experienced enough hurt and pain from me, I couldn't bear to put you through more. I raised Sara and Jason with the help of my students and my parents. My father still likes Shaun more than he ever liked you, but my mother is a different story. She actually told me, before she died, that she wished I would've run away with you and been happy rather than stay here for this."

Sam couldn't hide his surprise.

"I told Jason the truth when he was seven years old, and I gave him your note. He hated me for a long time afterwards. Sara was the one who finally helped me patch things up with him. She's an amazing young woman and if it hadn't been for her, I would have gone crazy long ago. My mom was right. I should have given everything up and sailed away with you and Jason. I was a fool not to have married you when you asked."

Sam took another sip from his drink. "Do you love him?" he asked, fearful of her answer.

She stepped closer to him and looked into his eyes. "I have only loved one person my whole life. Even when Shaun and I were together, it was you on my mind. I never stopped loving you."

Sam didn't think about his next action. He pulled her to him and kissed her deeply and passionately. She returned his passion, holding him close. Sam suddenly remembered she was still married to another man. It took all of his willpower to pull away from her. "I shouldn't have done that," he said, avoiding her eyes. "You're still a married woman."

"It's good to know some people never change. You still believe in honor, after all you've been through."

Sam nodded, trying to calm his urge to take her away with him. "A person can survive the loss of everything except his honor. I still love you, Macy, I never stopped loving you, even though I was angry. If you were free, I would take you away from here now and we would live out the rest of our lives together. But you're not and I can't behave the way I did today."

"Will you at least be my date for tonight? Shaun refused to come to the wedding, because I wouldn't come out to the beach for one of his stupid parties."

"I could never turn down a date with you," he said, offering his arm.

They rejoined the reception and Macy introduced him to many of her friends and coworkers. Timber and her husband were there, excited to see them together again. "Now you can get rid of that jerk you married and be with the one you were meant for," Timber told her loud enough for Sam to hear.

When the DJ began to play, Jason and Angela were the first dance, followed by Jason, Macy, Angela and her father. Jason was surprised to see his parents together when he went to get his mom.

"This is a pleasant sight," he said, offering her his arm. He made sure to return her to his father when the song was done. Sam waited until the next slow song to ask Macy to dance. She smiled and let him take her out on the dance floor while the music played.

"It has been a long time since I've danced, remember that little place in Costa Rica where we learned how to salsa?"

Sam laughed at the memory. "I do, and I remember being really bad at it."

She laughed with him. "You weren't bad at all; it was your dance partner who kept stepping on your toes who was terrible."

The song ended too soon for both of them and they retired to a table in the back yard near the dance floor. Sara was fending off a small group of young men who were asking her to dance. Macy tried in vain to hide her smile when she and Sam approached.

"She looks like she could use a rescue," Macy said to Sam.

"Are you suggesting a dashing sea captain should come to the aid of a damsel beset by land sharks?"

Macy chuckled at the analogy. "That is exactly what I'm suggesting, my dashing sea captain."

Sam winked at her and detoured toward the table where Sara was besieged.

"Excuse me, gentlemen, but the lady has promised an old man the first dance on her card," he said, stopping behind them. "Because I am stealing her away, please allow me to buy all of you a round at the bar."

The four men who surrounded her beamed at the offer of free drinks and headed in the direction of the bar. Sam offered his hand to her and led her toward the dance floor.

"Thank you, but you do know the bar is free tonight, don't you?"

"I do, but I don't think they know," he said while they swayed to the music. "Macy noticed the flock of seagulls hovering around you and asked if I would help."

"I'll have to remember that one. I'm sorry for taking you away from her. I know it's been a while since you two have been together. She misses you a lot."

Sam wasn't sure how to respond to her. "I'm sure she cares for your father, too," he said, trying to sound convincing.

Sara laughed and shook her head. "No, she doesn't and neither do I." Sam was surprised. "The only smart thing my father ever did was leave me with Macy. Macy's an extraordinary woman and has led the most interesting life. I used to be jealous of her and Jason, because they had someone who cared so much for them. Macy would sit and look through old pictures with us and tell stories about you to Jason. I used to pretend you were also my father and I wished she would take us to meet you on your ship so we could sail off and be a family." She laughed at herself. "I guess it was just the foolish wishes of a little girl."

"I'm sorry for what your dad put you through. I have to confess, I didn't think much of him the one time I met him. But I couldn't tell Macy without sounding like the jealous boyfriend."

She laughed at the thought. "For my sake, I'm glad you didn't come between them, or I would never have grown up to be who I am today."

"What are you doing now?"

"I'm in my final year of school here at Duke and majoring in Business law. I'm hoping to find a job somewhere and get out of North Carolina after graduation." Sam asked about her grades. "I have a 3.8 GPA with two semesters to go," she told him before the song ended.

They walked back to the table where Jason, Angela, and Macy were sitting. While they were sitting together, a photographer came over and took a group picture. Jason and Angela eventually had to leave and they ran through a shower of bird seed to reach the limo waiting in the front yard. The party began to wind down afterwards and eventually there were only a few people left.

"So where are you staying?" Macy asked Sam at the end of the night.

"I have a hotel room in the city."

"You could stay with me. You can have Jason's old room, if you want it."

Sam thought about it for a moment and finally shook his head.

"That wouldn't look good, for your old lover to stay at your house while your husband is away," he said, fighting the urge to take her offer.

She looked a little disappointed. "Are you sure?" she asked, moving closer to him.

He took a deep breath and nodded. "I'm sure."

"Well, the least I could do is give you a lift to your hotel."

Because they had both been drinking, she called a cab to take them back to Raleigh. He gave the cabbie her address for the first stop and asked him to wait while they said goodnight at the door. He longed to kiss her again, but settled for a hug and a kiss on the cheek. He went back to his hotel and took a long cold shower before going to bed.

The ringing of his satellite phone woke him the next morning.

"Are you busy? Because I could use some breakfast and a little company," Macy told him.

He checked the time before he answered. "I can grab some breakfast, but I'm due to fly out a little after lunch."

"Tell me where you are and I'll meet you there in a little while. I'll also make sure you get to the airport on time."

They met at an International House of Pancakes for breakfast, a block down the street from his hotel.

"Are you sure you have to leave so quickly?" she asked him after they ordered. "It's been so long since I saw you I would like to spend some time with you."

He smiled, tempted by the idea, but shook his head. "I have to get back for the christening of the newest addition to my fleet. The cruise side of the business has taken off and we have to grow to meet demand."

She took him to the airport and walked with him to the departure gate. They sat and talked while waiting on his flight to be called.

"Why does it always end like this for us?" she asked.

He shook his head sadly. "I don't know."

The attendant called his flight number.

She gave him a long hug and a quick kiss on the lips. "Don't be a stranger."

"Keep in touch."

Sam walked to the gate and glanced back to see her watching him. He gave a short wave which she returned, before heading down the ramp to the airplane that would separate them again.

Chapter 9

Charlotte Amalie was now in sight and the sun was falling toward the horizon. He was tired and hungry but he didn't stop to rest or eat. He sailed toward the airport and pulled up to a marina in Druif Bay. He secured the lines on the boat and walked up the dock to find the harbor master. He ordered enough food to get him through the rest of his trip and asked for his fresh water tanks to be refilled.

"How long will you be staying with us?" the harbor master asked.

"Overnight, I just need a place to shower and wash some clothes."

The harbor master showed him where the washing machines were located and left him to his work. The old man put on a load of clothes then sat to wait. He dozed off and entered his dreams again.

Jason stood next to him on a quay in Miami. Sara stood on a platform that was up to Sam's shoulder. She was holding a bottle of Champaign for the christening of a new vessel. They were all dressed in the Island Breeze Sailing Company dress uniform: white pants and shirts, with navy ties and jackets with gold buttons and braiding on the sleeves. A small flock of reporters and a larger group of spectators, stood under the warming morning sun to watch and record the event. The ship was brand new and had been designed as a passenger liner. She was longer than the ships he normally sailed and slightly taller. It had six roomy staterooms for guests, berths for the crew below the waterline, a world class galley with an award-winning chef and a fully-staffed dining room. Powered by sail, the *Alabama* boasted a unique experience for its passengers. Glancing at his watch, Sam stepped behind the small podium to speak.

"Welcome, everyone, to the christening of our newest ship." The photographers snapped photos, capturing him as he spoke. "Please allow me to introduce a few of the people who are an integral part of the line and the operations of the ship. First is Captain Doug Stephens, who will command the ship and crew. Doug has served as my First Mate for twelve years and captained the *Georgia* on her maiden cruise. Beside him is Marko Wade, Captain Stephens' First Mate. Up on the platform is Miss Sara Harrison, the operations manager for our cruise line and the person responsible for the reception later today. Last but not least, is Jason Richards, the Operations Manager for the cargo side of the business. His hard work will allow me to focus on growing the company and opening new ports of call. Now I will turn it over to Miss Harrison for the Christening."

Sam handed her the microphone and stepped into line behind Jason. Sara drew back the bottle and smashed it against the bow announcing, "I christen this sailing vessel *The Alabama*!"

A reception was held afterwards so the media and others could tour the ship. Sam stood next to Doug in the receiving line on the main deck at the head of the gangplank, welcoming their guests. He was speaking to a reporter when his cell phone rang. He excused himself from the line and answered.

"Sam, it's Macy, Uncle Jack is very sick and he's asking for you."

Sam was stunned. "What's going on?" he asked. "Where is he?"

"He had a stroke and he's here at the medical university. Lynn and the boys are waiting with me, but he's asking for you."

Sam looked over to where Sara and Jason were greeting the guests.

"Alright, I'm coming and bringing the kids with me."

"Thank you."

Sam put his phone away and hurried over to where Doug was in line.

"Doug, may I have a minute?" he asked. They crossed the deck to a more private spot before Sam explained what was going on. "Can you manage this on your own?"

Doug chuckled. "I don't see where I would have any problems. Sara has everything well planned and between Marko and me, I think we can figure it out,"

Sam looked relieved. "That's why I made you Captain. Now for the hard part," he said, walking over to where Jason and Sara were standing.

He pulled them aside and explained what was going on. "I will see about a flight and meet you at the office in an hour. I need to stop by the boat to get some clothes before I can go."

The three of them slipped off the ship. After packing everything they would need, they met at the office. Angela was with Jason, but Sam prepared her a reserved seat on the flight. She was pregnant with his first grandchild and moved slowly, but she refused to stay behind. The flight was only two hours and after a short cab ride to the medical university, they headed inside. Macy hugged him when he found her in the waiting room. Jack's two sons came over to speak with him before they led Sam to their father's room. Lynn was sitting beside Jack and looked up when Sam walked in.

"You came," she said hugging him. "Thank you."

Sam saw that Jack was asleep and spoke softly. "How is he doing?"

Lynn looked at him with tears filling her eyes. "The doctor said with a lot of therapy he might be able to use his right arm and leg again. But he has to get through the next 48 hours first."

Sam couldn't believe it. Jack opened his eyes and looked at the two of them.

"Hey, Jack," Sam said with a smile.

Jack held out his left hand. Sam could see the frustration in Jack's face when he tried to talk. "God to ee ewe."

"It's good to see you too, Jack," Sam said before he turned to Lynn. "Why don't you take a break and I'll sit with him for a few minutes." Lynn hesitated until Jack nodded at her to indicate it was okay. Once Lynn was gone, Jack looked at Sam and spoke.

"Am, I eed fabor ewe," Jack said, with effort. "When am doan, wunt ewe be exector."

"Jack, I'm honored, but you won't need an executor for a long time."

Jack shook his head. "Am, dis it for me, tank ewe."

Sam felt a tightness in his chest as Jack spoke. "Thank me for what?" Sam asked.

Jack tried to smile but only half of his face worked. "For share ewe wuv of wife with me, my boys. Sho den ow chase dreans."

"I'm still chasing one of them."

Jack turned serious. "On't ive up."

Lynn came back to check on them and Jack squeezed Sam's hand.

"She ewe my fend," Jack said with a tear in his eye. Sam smiled, holding back a tear of his own.

"See you soon, Jack."

Sam found everyone else in the waiting room. Sara and Jason wanted to know how their uncle was.

"He's resting and can't move his right side. Lynn is taking care of him. He's tough, he'll be fine," Sam said, not really believing it himself.

Macy could see the real truth in his eyes, and then hung her head in disappointment.

"Michael, Mark, why don't you take Jason and Sara to the house so they can put their bags away," Macy suggested.

They left, though they didn't want to go. When it was just Macy and Sam in the waiting room she turned to him.

"He told you he was dying, didn't he?" Sadly, Sam nodded yes.

She let out a long breath. "He told me the same thing, though he didn't say anything to Lynn or the boys," She reached over and held his hand. "I'm glad you came. For Jack's sake and mine."

Sam squeezed her hand gently. "I'll always come when you call. No matter the cost."

They kept a vigil at the hospital all night. Sam learned that Michael and Mark had both gotten their pilot's license and were working dusting crops for the family.

"We caught the flying bug from you and dad. Not to mention the girls think it's sexy, at least those who like the smell of chemicals and fertilizer."

Sam laughed hard at that one. Around midnight, Macy fell asleep wrapped in a blanket, leaning against Sam's shoulder. The boys were asleep on the floor, but Sam couldn't rest. Jason, Angela, and Sara had gone to the house to rest from the trip and would be in early the next morning, to give Sam and Macy a break from the hospital. Lynn appeared in the doorway of the waiting room and catching Sam's attention. He could tell what happened by the look on her face.

"He's gone," she said sadly.

She sat next to Sam and he put his arm around her. "I'm sorry, Lynn."

She cried on his shoulder while he rubbed her back. Macy awoke, saw Sam comforting Lynn, and knew her uncle was dead. Sam held them both while they cried softly. Lynn looked at her boys and watched them sleeping peacefully.

"I hate to wake them up and tell them."

Sam rubbed her shoulder. "I'll do it."

"You don't have to."

Sam smiled at her while Macy wiped her eyes. "Go with Macy to say goodbye. I'll bring the boys in a few minutes."

"You've been a good friend to us, Sam. Jack loved you like a brother, so do the rest of us," Offering him a little comfort before Macy led her from the room.

Sam took a moment to steel himself for the boys. He shook them gently and they awoke quickly.

"What's happened?" Michael asked.

"Guys, your mom needs you and she needs you to be strong for her."

Mark knew what he was saying and he rubbed at his eyes. Michael saw his brother's reaction and broke into tears.

"He's gone?" he asked Sam.

"I'm afraid so. Take a few minutes, Macy's with your mom. We can go to the room when you're ready."

Sam walked them to the room a few minutes later and let them go ahead of him. Jack was lying there peacefully, the boys gathered around the bed. Sam took a deep breath battling his emotions and Macy came over slipping her arm around him. He put his arms around her and his tears flowed. One of the nurses came in and Sam quickly wiped his wet face with the back of his hand.

"We need to take him now."

"Give us another moment, please."

Macy reached up and kissed him on the cheek. "I'll get our stuff together," she whispered, letting him go and heading for the waiting room.

Sam told Lynn it was time to go and rest. He would stay until Jack was taken away. She agreed and Sam had Michael lead her out of the room. Mark followed them out and left Sam alone with Jack. "Goodbye, my friend. You have my word that I'll take care of your family."

On his way out, he stopped to talk with the nurse. "Here is my number if there is anything that needs to be taken care of."

She added it to a folder with Jack's name on it saying, "We'll take good care of him."

They all went back to Macy's house in her SUV. Sam told Sara, Jason, and Angela what happened and recommended everyone get a few hours of sleep. Sara and Macy took Lynn to Macy's room to rest, while Jason gave the boys his room. Sam walked out into the back yard and sat in a lounge chair next to the pool. He leaned back in the chair and let his emotions run out. He didn't remember falling asleep, but he had been going for over thirty hours and was exhausted. The sounds of birds singing woke him and he found someone had covered him with a blanket. He stretched his tired muscles and headed inside, Jason was awake and had made coffee. Sam poured a cup and joined his son at the table.

"You okay?" Sam asked.

Jason looked at his father and shrugged in reply. "I'm fine, Dad. I couldn't sleep so I got up. Angela is still resting."

Sam sipped at his coffee. "Who do I have to thank for the blanket?"

"Mom; she thought you had gone until she found you by the pool."

"No, I just needed a few minutes alone."

Macy walked in looking tired. She poured a cup of coffee and sat across from Sam.

"Thanks for the blanket."

She smiled over her coffee. "Didn't want you to get cold out there."

"I'm kind of used to sleeping under the stars, but it's a bit cooler up here, so thanks. How's Lynn?"

"She'll be alright, but right now she's barely holding it together."

"The boys seem to be doing better."

Lynn walked in and joined them. She looked at Sam and let out a long sigh. "I guess we have to make arrangements for Jack."

Sam reached out and took her hand. "Only when you're ready and feel up to it."

She smiled and squeezed his hand. "I can do this; I have to for the boys."

Macy put a cup of coffee in front of Lynn and sat down. "I'll call the funeral home and see what time they can meet with us," she told her aunt.

Lynn nodded in silence and stared at her coffee.

A few hours later, before lunch, Sam, Macy, Lynn, and the boys met with the funeral home and made the arrangements. They returned to Macy's house for Lynn to rest and everyone to eat. There were cars parked along each side of the street when they arrived. When they walked inside, Angela and Sara were entertaining a crowd of people who had come to pay their respects. Sam let Macy and the boys run interference while he took Lynn to Macy's room to rest.

"You don't have to see anyone until you're ready. Let the boys visit for now and you just rest until you feel like coming out."

Sam left Lynn and was heading back toward the den when he heard Macy talking to someone in a strained tone. He rounded the corner to find Shaun Harrison standing in front of a crowd, trying to hug Macy. Sara had a stricken look on her face while Jason was ready to explode.

"What are you doing here, Shaun?" Macy asked, her expression switching between annoyance and worry. "You never come here."

Shaun shrugged his shoulders, reveling in the attention they were drawing. "I came to make sure you were okay," he said without a hint of sincerity. "Besides, I still live here."

Macy looked ready to punch him. Shaun picked up his bag and started toward the hall where Sam stood.

"Aunt Lynn is resting in my room; don't disturb her," Macy warned, not seeing Sam blocking the hall.

"I just want to pay my respects and put my bags in our room." He turned back and nearly ran into Sam, who stood in the hall entrance. "Oh, I see now why you were so interested in why I was here. Hello, Captain, or is it Admiral now? The sea spit you out on my doorstep at last?" he said, never taking his eyes off Sam. "Have you moved your stuff into her room yet? I bet you didn't expect her husband to show up, did you?"

Sam's eyes went dark while his rage built. "Shaun, Lynn is resting and you aren't going to disturb her."

Shaun laughed. "You're not going to tell me what to do in my house. Now move, before I move you."

Sam stepped closer to Shaun, unafraid of his threat. "I'll take your bag, but you're not going to bother Lynn."

The two men stood, nose to nose, locked in a battle of wills each was determined to win. Sam's calm demeanor was in contrast with Shaun's spiteful sneer. Shaun decided against pushing past Sam to see how he'd react.

"Fine, take my bags, boy, I should comfort my wife anyway."

Sam grabbed the bag, catching Shaun's hand around the handle and squeezing hard. Yanking his hand away, Shaun reached into his pocket, holding out a dollar.

"There's a tip for you, bellhop, I'd like the sheets turned down before bed," he said, dropping the bill on the floor.

Sam picked up the suitcase leaving the money lying on the floor. He put the suitcase beside the door in the hall, and then rejoined the rest of the family, staying close to the entrance to the hall.

Jason met him with a plate of food and some sweet tea. "You should have planted him; he was being an ass."

Sam shook his head. "Now's not the time or the place, as much as I might agree with you. I'll not dishonor Jack's memory."

Sara rushed over and looked at Sam with a horrified expression. "Sam, I'm so sorry about that."

He held up his hand to stop her. "Sara, a small bruise to my pride is all it was; bringing attention to it only makes it a bigger deal than it was and that's what he wants, that and to make me look bad. I know he's your father and because of that, and the fact he's still Macy's husband, he gets a pass for now."

Sam excused himself and went to check on Michael and Mark. Macy returned from the kitchen and saw him talking but didn't interrupt. Shaun returned to the room with a mixed drink and began talking loudly. Sam kept his distance from Shaun and each time Shaun would try to join the group Sam was talking with, Sam would politely slip away. It was later in the evening when everyone was gone; Sam had to get out for some peace and quiet. He silently slipped out the back door and sat by himself in the pool house where Jason discovered him later.

"Hey, Dad, Aunt Lynn was asking where you went."

"Tell her I'll be inside in a few minutes. I just needed to get some air."

"Angela said you must have the patience of a saint to put up with Shaun without killing him. I agree. I must have gotten mom's patience instead of yours because I've wanted to smack him ever since he showed up."

"I'm afraid you have it backward. My temper is much worse than your mother's. I've just had a lifetime of learning to control it. Do me a favor and bring my sea bag out here, please. It'll make things easier on your mom."

Sam followed him inside and found Lynn beset my Shaun. Spotting Sam when he walked in, Lynn got up and left Shaun sitting there, crossing to where Sam waited.

"I can't stand him another minute."

"How about letting me take you and the boys out for dinner?"

Lynn went to find her sons.

Sam turned to find Macy watching him. "I'm going to take Lynn away from here for a while and let her relax. We'll be back later."

"I'll wait up."

Sam shook his head. "Visit with your husband and don't worry about us."

Sam took them out to eat and gave Lynn several drinks to help her relax. They talked about Jack and his flying until it was time to get back. Sam returned to the house, determined to make sure they got past Shaun without him bothering them. Shaun was passed out on the couch in the den, drunk, a half empty drink on the coffee table. Macy took Lynn into the bedroom while Sam headed for the pool house. He stretched out in a recliner on the sectional and felt sadness for his friend. The sliding glass door opened and he heard Macy call his name.

"Sam, you in here?"

"Yeah, I figured it would cause fewer problems if I was out of sight."

It was dark in the room, but he could see her outline in the lights from the house.

"I haven't gotten a chance to talk to you since Shaun got here. I was proud of your control today." She sat beside him.

"It seems everyone really wanted me to knock him out, instead of walk away. But it's his house and I'm sure me being there didn't sit well with him."

"Shaun was pretty pissed about it. I'm glad you didn't hear that conversation." Sam didn't reply. After a few minutes of silence, she asked, "Are you alright?"

"I'm fine. But I do miss the old man."

She put her hand on his knee. "I know you do; he loved you and I know you cared for him the same way. You have been good for Lynn and the boys. Jack always said you were the best person he knew."

Sam smiled in the darkness. "He was a good friend and a good man."

Macy was quiet for a minute. "I've decided, after the funeral, I'm divorcing Shaun," she said out of the blue. Sam didn't say anything. "His behavior today was more than I could take. I should've done this a long time ago, but I was too stupid to see he would never change."

Sam let out a deep breath. "Tomorrow will be an emotional day; you should get some rest."

She hesitated, and then stood. "Goodnight, Sam."

Sam let her go without a word. He was emotionally shot and couldn't deal with her, Shaun, and everything else right now. For the first time since he arrived he wished he was back at sea again. Things were simple there: problems came up and they were handled, not like his personal life where things seemed to stay broken. The emotions and his grief overwhelmed him, bringing on the sleep he needed. His dreams were filled with snapshots of Jack, making him sleep fitfully all night.

Sam helped Lynn and her boys through the visitation the next night without having a confrontation with Shaun, but it was getting harder. Sam's nerves were shot by the time of the funeral and his temper was running short. Shaun was taking every shot he could at Sam without confronting him directly. Everyone saw it and wondered when Sam was going to reach his limit, but he maintained control of his temper. The funeral was sad and Lynn leaned on Sam for support through the service. Her boys did as well and Sam was glad he could be there for them. After the funeral, Lynn and the boys were ready to go home. Sam had received enough abuse between Macy's father and Shaun during the visitation and funeral. Sam needed to get some distance between them before he lost the little control he had left. He helped the family pack then took them out to their house on the McCoy farm Jack built.

"You're welcome to stay with us," Mark told him. "It will at least get you away from Shaun and out of the pool house."

"I'll be back, but I'm only staying for a few more days, I have to get back to work soon."

Sam left them at the house and went back to Macy's. Shaun was sitting in the front yard drinking beer when he pulled up.

"You came back for more?" Shaun asked in a slurred voice. Sam smiled at him and walked past him without a word. He went to the pool house and packed his sea bag. He was walking through the house on the way to the car when Macy stopped him.

"Leaving already?"

"Mark and Michael asked me to stay out at the farm and help with Lynn. I'm only here for a few more days, and then I'm heading back to work." She was sad at the news. "Will you please tell Jason and Sara where I'll be?"

She nodded and walked him to the door. She hugged him saying goodbye. "Thank you for everything you've done for Lynn," she said, stopping at the door.

Shaun looked over and laughed. "The sailor boy's leaving you, again? Should I close my eyes while you kiss him goodbye, or are you meeting him later?"

"You are such an asshole, Shaun," Sam said as he walked past him.

Shaun threw a half empty bottle at Sam, hitting him in the back. "At least I'm not sleeping with another man's wife."

Sam spun around and, in two steps, grabbed Shaun around his neck in one hand, lifting him out of the chair and slamming him against the wall. Sam may have been in his fifties, but the hard work he'd done his whole life had hardened his muscles into steel. It happened so fast that Shaun didn't even move until his head bounced off the wall.

"Listen up, jerk," Sam said, letting his anger escape. "I could have had your wife anytime I wanted her, but I'm a gentleman and refused to take advantage of the situation. If you actually knew me, you'd know I would never violate someone's marriage. I held my peace out of respect for Jack and his family, but I've had enough. One more word out of you and the only thing that will beat you to the hospital is the lights of the ambulance. Are we clear?"

Shaun tried to claw at Sam's hand to get free, but Sam held him like a vice. "We're clear," Shaun gasped, finally realizing he was over-matched.

"Good decision. I'm leaving and I won't be back. So, if you don't look for me, I won't go looking for you. It'll be better for you if you just leave me alone. Make no mistake, Shaun. If you cause Macy any grief, you won't like what happens."

Sam turned Shaun loose, letting him fall to the ground. He stomped across the yard to the car he'd borrowed from Mark. He drove away, struggling to calm his emotions. He was angry at himself for letting his control slip, even though he knew Shaun deserved more than he'd done.

He'd calmed by the time he arrived at Jack's house. He was getting out of the car when his phone rang.

"Mr. Richards?" the voice asked.

Sam furrowed his brow as he replied, "Speaking."

"Mr. Richards, this is Frank Johnson at the shipyard in Norfolk. The last ship in your order is ready. We finished early and it only needs a shakedown cruise or your approval for us to release it."

"Sounds good. I'm in Raleigh, North Carolina, at the moment and will be here for a few more days. I can be there by Wednesday to take a look at her."

"Sounds good. I look forward to seeing you then."

"Good, I will see you on Wednesday."

Mark walked onto the porch while he was talking. "Where you headed?" Mark asked.

Sam smiled, walking up the steps with his bag on his shoulder. "Norfolk; my new ship's ready and needs a sea trial."

"That would be cool to see."

They stopped at the door. "Why don't you, your brother, and your mom come with me? You could be my personal guests and I'll even fly you home when we reach Key West."

"It would be cool, if I could talk mom into it. Mike's gonna flip when I tell him," Mark said as he went inside.

Sam called Sara and told her about the conversation. "I'll call Solomon and see how soon he can have a crew there. Give me a few hours and I'll call you back," Sara told him. She quickly caught Solomon up on her conversation with Doug, assuring him all was well with his fleet.

He was cooking dinner when she called him back. "Solomon said the crew would be there Friday. That's the fastest he can get them there unless you want to fly them in. We have a freight shipment going north so they'll hitch a ride with them."

Sam thought for a minute. "Alright, I'll let Frank know he has an extra day."

"Hey, there's one more thing: Daddy's filing assault charges against you and wants you arrested."

Sam took a deep breath and let it out. "Thanks for the heads up. Don't worry about it; just get me a crew for the ship. I'll take care of the rest."

He hung up and took a moment to think. Michael walked in and saw him standing there with a grimace on his face.

"Are you okay?" Michael asked. Sam snapped out of his trance and smiled.

"I'm fine, but I might have to move up my plans for leaving. Seems I'm a wanted man now," Sam said with a chuckle. Mark walked in, in time to hear the last part.

"Wanted for what?"

Sam told them about the episode with Shaun.

"Sara just let me know he wants to press charges."

Mark laughed. "Let him try. We're in a different county and the sheriff was a good friend of daddy's. I'll talk to him after supper and straighten this out. If not, we can fly you out of here in the duster."

"Who are you getting out of here and why?" Lynn asked while showing interest in Sam's cooking.

Mark told her the story while Sam fixed each of them a plate.

"I'll talk to the sheriff myself. Don't you worry about Shaun Harrison. I'll take care of him and smile doing it. Now what's this business about us going out on a ship?" she asked Sam when he handed her a plate.

Sam was at the reading of the will and the attorney explained to him what his role as executor required. Jack left envelopes for each of the people he was leaving his belongings to, making Sam's job easier. Shaun and Macy were there along with a few of Jack's friends who Sam met at the funeral. Sam received an envelope along with the rest of them. In his role of executor, he asked them to wait until Jack's will was read before opening them. Everything other than what was in the envelopes was left to Lynn and the boys. Jack's attorney finally announced everything was in order and they could open the contents of the envelopes. Sam waited until everyone read their notes inside from Jack, detailing what he wanted them to have and why. It was up to him to dispense the items and make sure they were delivered to the right person. The attorney had the items with him and helped Sam verify them while they gave out everything but one item. Everyone seemed happy with what they had received from Jack. Finally, Sam picked up his envelope and broke the seal. He read the letter in Jack's handwriting.

> *Sam, every sailor needs a place to call home, now you have yours. I hope one day you and Macy will be together and be as happy as Lynn and I have been.*

> *Jack*

Sam looked over to where the attorney was sitting and the man handed him a second envelope. Sam opened it and his eyes widened when he started reading. He shook his head slowly and looked at the lawyer.

"Is this right?"

The attorney looked it over quickly. "It appears to be in order."

"Son of a gun," Sam chuckled.

Lynn was watching him with a slight smile, knowing what was in the letter and the other envelope. Mark, throwing his manners to the wind, looked over his shoulder and saw it was a deed.

"Dad gave you some property here? Are we going to be neighbors?" Mark asked excitedly.

Sam shook his head. "No, this address is on Hatteras Island." He looked at Lynn as she smiled with great pleasure.

She pointed at Shaun and smiled evilly. "It looks like you have a new landlord."

Macy looked like she was torn between laughing and crying, her hands covering her mouth. Sam shook his head, staring at the document. "Unbelievable, the man was insane."

Included with the documents was a Notice of Eviction, which Sam handed to Shaun. Shaun was furious and stormed out of the room without a word. Lynn looked at Sam and winked.

"Chief Dandridge has been notified and will be keeping an eye on the place until he's gone," she told him. "The eviction notice is effective immediately."

"You knew about this?" he asked, then thought about it. "Of course, you did, Jack always ran things like this though you."

"Right on both counts. He hoped by now, you would be ready to settle down. He wanted you to have a place that meant something to you. He bought it back from Macy, who wasn't using it anyway, now it's yours."

"I've never owned a house before," he said, still in shock.

Macy laughed from the other side of the table. "I wondered why Jack wanted it back so badly. I guess I should go see to Shaun."

She hugged Lynn and the boys but paused when she reached Sam.

"Maybe one day I can drop by and visit, if you're going to live there." She kissed him on the cheek and walked out of the door.

Before Sam could leave, Lynn told him she and her sons had enough to do running the farm and she didn't feel right going off so soon after Jack's death. He was sad they wouldn't be traveling with him, but he understood. Sam didn't see Macy again before he left for Norfolk. Sara went with him, while Jason and Angela flew back to Miami to check on the cargo side of the business. Solomon, a tall, deep-voiced Honduran, was waiting for them with a crew of young men and a few women from his village. Sam and Solomon met when one of Sam's original crew members brought Solomon onboard while they were in port.

Solomon was a teacher, but he didn't teach math or science the conventional way. He taught kids and teenagers how to sail and navigate, applying math and science. Sam had been so impressed with the man and his school, he and Solomon reached an agreement and Sam's ships became the graduate course for Solomon's students. Solomon beamed with pleasure seeing Sam approach. "Good to see you, Salty Mon," Solomon said in his deep bass voice. "I have for you a fine new crew for a fine new ship,"

"Hello again, my friend. Have you been on board yet?" Sam asked as they hugged quickly.

"I have studied her from here, but we have not been on board," Solomon explained.

They found Frank and he took them on a thorough inspection. Sam and Sara toured the ship with Frank while Solomon sent his crew into the sails to check everything. The schooner was a three-mast ship, built for the cruise business. It was built in the style of an old British Man 'O War, but with far more comforts for the people who would be sailing with them. Sam spent the rest of the morning climbing the rigging and inspecting everything. Throughout his inspection, Sara stayed beside him and he showed her what to look for, making sure to explain why it was important. When he was done, he met Solomon and received a report from the crew.

"They have not found anything of consequence," Solomon said.

Sam looked over at Frank, who was smiling widely.

"It looks like your people have done another exceptional job," Sam said happily.

"The tide is turning and she's ready for a sail. If you will allow, we have built three of these for you, but I've never been on one under full sail. Would it be too much for me to ask for a ride?"

Sam laughed. "Not at all, it will take us close to eighteen hours to reach Savannah, Georgia, where we will put into port for supplies. We can drop you off there if you like."

Frank pulled out his cell phone and made a quick call. He came back a moment later wearing a huge grin. "My wife is jealous, but I'm ready."

Sam turned to Sara. "Call for assembly and let's get this show rolling."

Sara looked at him in surprise. "Me?"

"You're the First Mate for the shakedown. You can do it: sound assembly and be loud," he said with a wink.

Sara looked scared to death but Solomon smiled at her and showed her how to work the Boson's Pipe. Minutes later the crew was gathered in front of the wheelhouse.

"Assembled as ordered, Captain," Sara said, looking pleased with herself.

Sam gave her a curt nod and looked out at the young faces of his crew.

"We're going for a little run down to Savannah, Georgia, and after replenishing there, we're heading for our home port of Miami for the official christening of the ship. Solomon tells me you're a fine crew and I believe him. Now let's show these ship builders how to handle their creation like true sailors."

The crew cheered briefly. "Miss Harrison will be the First Mate on the voyage and her orders are no different from mine. This is her first time as Mate, but I expect you to respect her and answer quickly. If there is any confusion about orders, ask for clarification. No question will be turned aside. Miss Harrison, make preparations for departure."

"Aye, Captain." He saw she was nervous when she stepped up beside him and looked at her crew. "Stand by on the mooring lines, stow the gangplank, then all hands aloft, prepare to make sail."

Sam watched the crew scurry to follow her orders. He stepped up to the wheel and waited. Solomon watched his people while they went about their orders. He was the Quartermaster and would be circulating around the crew, watching them closely, still teaching. The lines holding them to the dock were released and hauled aboard. Sam set the rudder so the outgoing tide would help turn the ship and point her toward the channel. Sara watched the prow of the ship while it turned and once it was pointed in the proper direction, she ordered two sails lowered from their yardarms. There was a surge felt throughout the ship when the wind filled the sails, pushing them forward.

Frank stood next to Sam, grinning like a school boy. "This is amazing."

Sam laughed, scanning the channel in front of him for traffic. "Wait until you see her under full sail; she's a thing of beauty."

They reached the head of the channel and cleared the bar a few minutes later. Sara ordered the Mizzen and the Gallants lowered. They picked up speed turning south, running before the wind. Sam offered to let Frank take the wheel. He showed him the compass and told him what heading to hold, then pulled the chart for their run and let Sara plot their course with one of the students. He nodded after he checked her work. She called out a course change and Sam checked the sail configuration. Seeing everything was in order, he sat back and enjoyed the ride. Sam volunteered to take the midnight watch and would handle the tricky channel of the Savannah River when they arrived. Sara was doing well and Solomon was there to keep an eye on her, so Sam went to the Captain's cabin to grab a few hours' sleep. He was awakened by the smell of something tantalizing cooking in the galley. He checked his watch and saw only two hours remained until his watch was to start. He went to the galley and found Jerome, the ship's cook, had a thick vegetable stew prepared. Sam took two bowls up to the wheelhouse, handing one to Sara.

"So, what do you think of being the captain?" he asked.

"There's a lot to keep track of," she replied. "But it's fun."

Sam chuckled. "It can be at times, but it is also a lonely way to live. This ship needs a name. Have any suggestions?" he asked her, changing gears.

"So far, you've named them all after Southern States. What State haven't you used yet?" she asked.

Sam thought for a minute. "Let's see, I have the *Carolina, Georgia, Kentucky* and *Virginia* on the cargo side, on the cruise side there is the *Tennessee, Alabama* and *Florida.*"

"What about *Texas*?" she asked.

Sam thought about it a moment, then nodded. "*Texas,* it is then. Notify the shipyard and the maritime authority. You'll need to message the Savannah Port Authority of our new name and ETA. We'll want dockage on the river front." He then called the ship's carpenter over and explained what he wanted. The man headed below to begin carving the name for the ship.

Sam checked the charts and noted their position. They were nearly even with the city of Myrtle Beach, South Carolina. Sam relieved Solomon and Sara, sending them to rest for a few hours. It was the wee hours of the morning when he spotted the familiar lighthouse on Tybee Island. Sam smiled and found an area outside of the shipping lane and away from the large container ships to anchor for the night.

"Hands aloft and reef the sails," he ordered.

The night crew raced into the rigging to drop the sails and secure the canvas. He checked the chart again to make sure there were no wrecks close and enough water under the keel. Satisfied all was well, he ordered the anchors dropped. The ship settled and swayed gently at anchor in the warm breeze. He posted an anchor watch and called the harbor control to send a pilot after sunrise.

"The way is clear, you can motor in," the man instructed.

Sam laughed. "I would, but we don't have a motor, we're a sailing ship."

At dawn, a boat with PILOT written across the side, approached and the lookout called to let Sam know. The pilot boat pulled up to the Jacob's ladder on the starboard side and held its position while a man scrambled aboard.

"Permission to come aboard?" the man asked, poking his head over the edge of the deck.

"Granted," Sam said with a smile.

The pilot strode toward the quarterdeck where Sam waited, inspecting the crew and the ship on his way.

"This is marvelous. I've always dreamed of seeing one of these up close, but I never thought I would. John Douglas," he said, introducing himself.

"Captain Sam Richards, at your service. If you'll give me a few minutes to change the watch, we can raise anchor and head for port."

Solomon walked out of the main hatch and looked around, taking in the sail configuration and the crew at work.

"Solomon, will you please blow the change of watch?" Sam asked. Solomon pulled out a boson's whistle and played a short series of notes which could be heard throughout the ship. Sam checked his watch against the ship's clock mounted on the bulkhead behind him.

"Mr. Golder, sound seven bells, if you please." The young man rang the ship's bell seven times when the clock showed seven o'clock.

The crew moved to change watches, with those below, hustling up to the deck and relieving the night watch. The crew who were off duty milled around to watch the run into port. The bystanders were careful to stay out of the way of their counterparts or lend a hand where needed. Sara came up looking well-rested and carrying a cup of coffee for Sam.

"Morning, Captain," she said, handing him the cup. "Jerome will have breakfast prepared by the time we reach port. He wanted to bring it up so he could watch our run up the river."

"Very well, thank you," he said before introducing their pilot. "Let's get the sails ready and have the men stand by on the capstans."

Sara was more confident this time, shouting her orders to the crew. Seeing an opportunity to show off their skill, the crew raced up the ratlines and rapidly readied the sails. Sam smiled at their crispness, granting a nod to Solomon on his choice of crew.

"Mr. Douglas, if you would take the wheel, we can get underway. Set the rudder for 180 degrees, then the ship is yours, sir,"

The man was shocked that Sam would let him take the wheel.

"Aye, Captain," he said as he moved to the large ship's wheel, replacing the young sailor, who stepped aside, but not too far away.

Sara ordered the anchors raised. The ship moved with the tide flowing into the mouth of the Savannah River. Sara gave the orders for the sails with Solomon's assistance, while Sam watched, keeping an eye on the crew, the sails, the wind and the tide, all while calmly sipping his coffee. Frank stood at the rail near Sam, watching with a wide grin etched across his face. Jerome brought Sam a bowl of grits with butter and two slices of bacon. Sam thanked him, inviting the cook to watch the proceedings from the quarterdeck. They sailed past the guns of Fort Pulaski and Sam wished he'd installed a small signal cannon to salute the three-hundred-year-old fort. He paused to admire the courage it took the old gun runners who had once tried their luck racing past the fort's cannons. Nearing the docks on River Street, Sam took the wheel and issued orders to the crew. Douglas had two tugboats standing by to take the lines and assist them, but Sam waved them away. He used the tide to float the ship close to the place where he would dock.

"Reef all sail and stand by on the messenger lines," he shouted, judging the movement of the ship and the distance to the dock. When he felt close enough he shouted orders again. "Drop all sheets and cast off the messenger lines!"

Dock workers along the pier grabbed the lines, pulling the thicker main lines around the large cleats anchored to the pier. Above the deck, the crew secured the sails, cutting their speed drastically. Sam worked the wheel moving the ship close to the pier until it gently touched the tire bumpers lining the concrete dock.

"Secure the lines and ready the gangplank," he ordered. "Miss Harrison, assemble the crew, if you will."

Mr. Douglas shook his head in wonder. "There are container ship captains with years of service who couldn't have managed what you just did without a tug or an engine, that's real seamanship. Extremely well done, Captain."

"Thank you, but this isn't the first time I've done this." Sam replied.

"Captain, the crew is assembled and all lines are secure," Solomon reported.

"Excuse me, Mr. Douglas," Sam said, stepping up to the rail and looking at his crew. "Crew of the *Texas*," he said loud enough to be heard. "You have exceeded my expectations for so young a crew. We'll be here until tomorrow afternoon's outgoing tide. Sara will have the watch posted by the end of breakfast. We'll need all hands for the replenishment operation, but once we're situated, each watch will be granted liberty." There was a cheer from the young crew. "Take care and stay together, enjoy the port of Savannah, but not too much, I'd hate to leave anyone behind. That is all."

Solomon grinned at him. "I will see to the stores, Captain."

"Thank you, old friend," Sam said. "Sara, we will only need a fire watch posted. Make sure everyone gets some time ashore before we leave, including Solomon and yourself. Savannah's a beautiful city; you should see some of it while we're here."

She headed for her cabin to set the watch schedule. Sam turned to the pilot who was standing near the stairs to the main deck. "Mr. Douglas, thank you for your assistance this morning."

"May I get a picture before I go?"

"I don't mind at all." One of the crewmen took several pictures with Mr. Douglas' phone before he left.

Frank laughed, standing at the rail, looking at the shops along River Street. "I've never been here before. My wife's been wanting to visit Savannah for a long time, but my schedule has kept me from bringing her."

"I grew up across the river," Sam said. "Savannah and Charleston are two of the prettiest cities on the East coast. I wish I had time to show them to you, but I have an appointment to keep away from the ship."

Sam pulled out his phone and after a brief conversation, reserved a flight for the man. "Your flight leaves just after lunch. It's a direct flight back to North Carolina."

Frank shook his hand. "Thank you for letting me come with you. It was quite an experience."

"Maybe next time you'll bring your wife and be our guest. You'll both love it."

Frank said goodbye and headed down the gangplank to find a taxi to the airport. It wasn't long before the crew started loading provisions for the trip to Miami. Solomon had everything under control, so Sam left him in charge, taking Sara to lunch. They ate at The Shrimp Factory, then Sam told her he had some personal business to take care of. She looked at him oddly before she remembered he was raised here.

"Can I come with you?" she asked. "It might be the only time I get to see where you grew up."

Sam thought for a moment, and then agreed. They caught a taxi to a rental car company and Sam rented a small car to take them forty miles north to the small town of Ridgeland, South Carolina. He saw how much the town had changed since he'd been gone. He showed Sara where he once lived, and then drove to the end of the road where a cemetery sat. He parked, and then went to visit his family plot. Sara stood silently while Sam visited his parents and grandparents' graves. He wiped his eyes when he stood and together they walked in silence to the car. He took her to the airport where he once learned to fly.

"I spent so much time here," he said, looking around at the new hangars and the planes. He pointed to an old hangar sitting alone near a row of newer ones.

"That used to be where I kept my plane. This was also where I would practice for air shows."

"You used to fly in air shows? I never knew that."

"I guess Macy never told you how we met." Sara shook her head, curious about their story. "I was out on Tybee with my best friend and saw her race in a small ketch. Her team finished second and I went over to talk to them. Her partner turned out to be a jerk and left her there, so I took her back to the place she was staying. We went to the awards dinner together, then hung out on the beach and she took me sailing for the first time. The next day, I took her up in my plane and the rest is history."

"I've never heard that story before. So, what made you stop flying?" she asked.

"It was a tough time for me. Macy had pushed me away, my best friend decided to get married and wanted out of the business, and then my parents and brother were killed in a car accident. It was one of the worst years of my life. I just didn't feel the same about flying anymore. I decided I needed a change in my life. I had plenty of money from all the shows I'd done, so I didn't have to work for a while. I headed for my sailboat and sailed down to the Bahamas where I met a guy who was captain of what is now the *Carolina*. A long night of drinking later, I bought the boat and started my own business. I sold the planes and split the money with my buddy, then sailed away from all the pain and bad memories."

While they were standing there talking, a motorcycle pulled up near them. It was only when the man removed his helmet Sam recognized his old friend.

"Alex!" Sam said hugging him. "How the hell are you?"

Alex ginned. "I'm doing good. I was watching the news this morning and saw some crazy man bring a sailing ship into Savannah. I figured it had to be you. I was heading that way when I spotted you out here."

Sam turned to introduce Sara. "Alex, this is one of my employees, Sara Harrison. Sara, this is my oldest friend, Alex Benton."

They shook hands and Alex cut his eyes at Sam. "I guess you finally gave up on Macy and found a younger one?"

"Sara is Macy's step daughter and currently the director of my cruise line. She's the acting First Mate on the ship you saw on the news."

"Well, I feel dumb. I should've known you wouldn't give up on something you wanted. My apologies, ma'am."

Sam grinned at his old buddy. "So how about coming over to Savannah and dining with me tonight on the ship? You can tour the ship and I'll feed you."

Alex chuckled. "How could I refuse an offer like that?"

Dinner turned out to be fun for the crew, with Sam and Alex reliving their teenage years and talking about Sam's flying career. Alex produced a picture album and Sara flipped through the pages asking questions about each picture. The last picture was of Sam after his last show.

"You look sad in this one. Was it because you were done with flying?"

Sam smiled looking at the picture. "No, I was lost and didn't know what to do next."

Alex chuckled. "Hey, remember the trip we made to the Bahamas on your sailboat? I think you tried to drink all the rum in the islands on that trip."

"I probably remember less than you do. I remember teaching you to sail on that trip. I'm glad I did or else we would have been in trouble. I'm really glad we went, but man it took a long time to recover."

"It was the last time we went on vacation together," Alex laughed. Sara gave him a questioning look.

"Why was it the last time?"

"When we got back, Sam's parents were in a wreck. He decided to finish the shows we had scheduled then quit. When we were finally done, I went to college, married my sweetheart, got a degree in Computer Design, and then started my own company."

"Yeah, while I was going back to drink the rest of the rum I'd missed on the first trip, Alex was making something of himself. He was always the smart one."

They sat out on the deck after dinner and enjoyed a bottle of brandy Sam had picked up in town.

"So, when are you leaving again?" Alex asked.

"Tomorrow afternoon."

"Why so soon? You should stay a while; it's been years since we've been this close to each other. I kind of like having my best friend around again."

"I bet your wife would love that. She'd be scared I'd haul you off on another three-month vacation."

Alex chuckled. "Yeah, but damn it's been good seeing you again."

They walked the deck and caught up. The crew respectfully left them alone to talk and joke around while they went about their business. When the ship's bell rang eleven o' clock, Alex told him he had to go. Sam hated to see his friend leave and told him so.

"Just don't be a stranger," Alex said. "Come back home every once in a while."

"I'll try."

Sam watched him walk away and blend into the crowd. He headed for his cabin with a heavy heart, but was intercepted by Solomon.

"There's something wrong with Miss Harrison. She won't come out of her room and she has the late watch."

"Thank you, Solomon; I'll take care of it immediately."

He went to the door of her room and knocked.

"Sara, let me in."

He heard her sobbing inside and knocked again.

"Sara, I'll have the carpenter take the door down if you don't open it," he told her flatly. He heard movement and a second later the door opened.

"Please leave me alone."

Sam shook his head. "That, I can't do. You're like family to me and your problems are my problems, too. But you're late for your watch and that's something I can't allow a senior officer to do. So, tell me what's going on to make you neglect your duty."

She looked at him with eyes full of hurt. "I want to, but I'm afraid of what'll happen. Promise me you'll listen and not go crazy."

Sam hesitated. Several things ran through his mind, but none of them would have caused her to act like this. "I promise to listen; whatever it is can be fixed."

She shook her head and sat on the side of her bed.

"While you and your friend were walking the deck, Mark called me."

Sam immediately thought something had happened to Lynn. "He told me Macy's in the hospital. She's in serious condition because she was beaten by my father."

Sam stood still as a statue, his jaw clenched until his teeth hurt.

"Dad's in jail and mom was about to go into surgery. Mark said he'd call me when he knew more."

Sam struggled to keep his emotions in check and offered a comforting hug to Sara instead.

"Thank you for letting me know. Go find Solomon and tell him I need to see him right away. I'll be in my cabin." Sam walked to his cabin and closed the door, trying to work out a plan of action in his head. He closed his eyes, forcing his anger back into the dark side of his soul. There would be a time and a place to let the beast out of its cage, but right now he needed a clear head. When he felt calm again, he picked up his phone to call Mark. He noticed three missed calls from Mark and one from Jason. He called Jason first.

"Stay there with Angela," he told his son. "She needs you to be there when the baby comes. I'm sending Sara with Solomon to Miami so we can put the ship into service. Sara can tell you who's deserving of being the captain, go with her recommendation."

Jason grunted. "What're you going to do?"

Sam paused for a moment as several thoughts ran through his mind. "I'm going to go see about your mom first, then, I'm going make sure this never happens again."

Sam landed in Raleigh several hours later, in the middle of a rainstorm. The raging weather matched the storm of emotions brewing inside his heart. Mark was waiting at the baggage claim.

"How is she?" Sam asked when they shook hands.

Mark looked into Sam's eyes and saw the anger there. "She has a fractured jaw, and both eyes are black. She had an enlarged spleen which the doctors had to go in and repair. Several cracked ribs, but thank God they didn't puncture a lung. A neighbor called the cops or he might have killed her. She's in rough shape, but she's tough, she'll be fine now with you here."

Sam accepted the information without a word.

"Where's Shaun?"

Mark hesitated for a moment on their way to his car.

"He's staying at her house. He posted bail while you were flying in."

Sam simply nodded getting into the car.

"Where to?" Mark asked him nervously.

"I need to see Macy."

Mark took him to the hospital, and although visiting hours were over, Sam was able to sneak past the nurses and find her room. Macy was sleeping when he slipped in the door and closed it behind him. Even in the dim light of the room, Sam could see the damage to her body. Her face was swollen and she had two black eyes that were closed while she slept, letting her body recover. His anger boiled up seeing the damage Shaun had done. He went over and put the chair next to her bed. He was sitting there when the nurse came in to check on her. "Sir, how did you get in here?"

Sam looked at her. "It doesn't matter. What matters is this woman gets the best care available."

"Sir, I'm going to have to ask you to leave."

Sam shook his head. "Miss, I'm not leaving her side. You can call the police or security if you want, but it's only going to cause you more work, because no one's going to remove me without a fight. You have my word, I won't get in anyone's way or cause any problems; I just want to be here for her."

The nurse knew she wouldn't win the argument. "Alright, but one problem and you're out." Sam agreed to her demands. The nurse checked Macy's vitals, and then left them alone.

Sam dozed off sometime during night and slept until the shift changed. The new nurse was a round black woman who'd evidently been warned about his stubbornness. Sam moved out of her way while she checked on her patient. Sam saw that it was nearly eight in the morning. His stomach growled while he tried to remember when he'd eaten last.

"I can bring you a spouse's meal when I bring her breakfast," the nurse offered.

"Thank you, but I would settle for a cup of coffee at the moment."

The big black woman chuckled. "There's a pot at the nurses' station, I made this morning, Sugar. I don't know about you, but I can't function without my coffee." He accepted her invitation and went to the nurses' station.

Sam was back quickly. Macy began to stir, opening her eyes slowly. Seeing Sam, she looked at him for a moment with tears forming in her eyes. She picked up a notebook and pen. She wrote, *I can't talk because my jaw is wired shut. How long have you been here?*

He read it and smiled. "I got in last night. The nurses were nice enough to let me stay once I told them that they would need a battalion of Marines to remove me."

She put her pen to the paper again. *I'm a mess; I didn't want you to see me like this.*

"Nothing could take away from your beauty, my love."

She shook her head sadly. *How did you know? How did you get here so fast?*

"Mark called Sara and she told me. I was in Savannah and caught a flight back. Sara was upset, so I sent her to meet Jason with the ship. They're waiting for me to let them know what's going on."

Promise me you won't go after Shaun.

Sam read it and took a deep breath. "That, I won't promise. He's out of jail and at your house. I won't go looking for him, but if I see him, he'll pay for this. How did this happen?"

She looked at him for a moment, and then shook her head.

"Macy-" he said slowly.

She wrote for a moment and then turned the page toward him. *I told Shaun I was leaving him and was going to go be with you and my children. He was quiet for a while, and then he just exploded into a rage. I'd never seen him so angry. After I went down he just continued kicking and punching. I blacked out and woke up in the emergency room.*

"I'm so sorry, Macy."

She reached out and took his hand. Sam held her hand gently, afraid she might break at his touch. He kissed her hand softly.

"I'm not leaving you, rest and get better, so I can take you home. I'll be here when you wake up."

He remained by her side for a week. Lynn and her boys, along with several of Macy's students, came by to relieve him, but he was only gone long enough to return a few calls and update the kids on her progress. Sam fed her, bathed her and pushed her around the hospital in a wheelchair until she was able to walk with him. She was released at the end of the week and told to take it easy. Macy had lost weight and a lot of her energy while she was down. She was becoming depressed and had stopped writing unless she needed something. Sam noticed and he talked to the doctor about what he wanted to do. The doctor set everything up for Macy's care then released her. Lynn was waiting for them at the entrance to the hospital and took them back to her house to recover. Sam stayed with her and slept in a chair beside her bed each night in case she needed anything. It took three weeks for her jaw to heal enough to open again. As soon as the doctor released her wired jaw and cleared her to begin speaking again, the first thing she did was kiss Sam.

"I've been waiting a long time for that," she said, making Sam and the doctor laugh.

"If you're feeling up to it, how about a little trip?"

She was curious about where they were going, but he refused to tell her where he was taking her. Sam packed up their things and he took her to the beach house. The house was much the same as he remembered, though Shaun had left it a mess. Sam called a cleaning company to come by and thoroughly clean the place. He bought new beds and had the old ones removed. They spent their first night alone together sleeping next to each other, holding hands.

Sam was up early the next morning and went out to sit on the deck. His phone rang and he answered it so it wouldn't wake Macy.

"Sam," Lynn said in a troubled voice. "Shaun was here looking for Macy. I told him she was out of town and I didn't know where she was. I think he figured it out though, because he mentioned something about a car trip."

Sam smiled. "Don't worry. He doesn't know I'm here, does he?"

"I didn't tell him anything about you."

"Then he'll be in for a nice surprise."

"Should I call the sheriff and have him standing by?"

"No, if there's trouble, I'll take care of it."

"How's Macy?"

"She's sleeping soundly and healing."

"Sam, she should go with you when you go back to the ship. I'll miss her, but she should be with you."

They talked for a few more minutes and said goodbye. Sam went back inside and saw Macy preparing breakfast.

"Hey," Sam said. "I can do that, you should be resting."

"You've been taking care of me for a month. It's my turn to take care of you."

He sat down to watch her cook. She made pancakes and coffee, but she moved slowly and Sam could tell she was still hurting a little. She picked at a pancake and sipped her coffee while he ate.

"Sam, I have something I want to talk to you about. It'll take a year for the divorce to go through and there's the court case. I know you'd like me to just pack up and go sailing off with you, but I can't do it until I settle things here. I owe the school a chance to find my replacement and I'll need to sell the house. I know it's disappointing to you, but it's the only way I can get closure on my life here." She wiped her eyes.

Sam reached out and held her hand. "You do whatever you need to do. I'll be there waiting."

She looked at him and shook her head. "I'd hoped you'd understand. You're amazing and far too good to me."

It was early evening when they heard hammering on the front door. Macy looked at Sam when she heard Shaun shout for her to open the door.

"Go upstairs and call the sheriff. Lock the bedroom door and only open it for me or the cops." She hesitated. "Go," Sam said firmly.

She started up the stairs and he made sure he heard the door close. Sam yanked open the door and faced off with Shaun.

"Where's my wife?" Shaun demanded.

Sam could smell alcohol on his breath. "Resting."

"I bet. Tell her to get her ass down here, she's coming with me."

Sam shook his head. "She's not leaving with you and I want you off my property."

Shaun tried to push his way past Sam.

"Macy!" Shaun yelled. "Get down here!"

Sam blocked his path. "Get out Shaun or I'll throw you out."

Shaun tried to hit Sam, but Sam saw the punch coming and blocked his arm. He sent a punch of his own into Shaun's stomach doubling him over. Sam grabbed Shaun shoving him out the door and across the porch. Shaun landed in a pile at the bottom of the porch steps.

"I guess it's different when someone fights back. Be glad I'm controlling my temper. You should leave before I decide to let you see what a real beating looks like."

Shaun got to his feet and pulled a small revolver from his pocket. He pointed it at Sam and laughed.

"It's different when you're on the wrong end of a gun," Shaun said taunting him. "Now, I'm looking for Macy and I'm not leaving until I see her. You can move or I can shoot you."

Sam lunged for the door and slammed it. BANG BANG BANG BANG BANG BANG! The door splintered with each shot peppering Sam with shrapnel. The stink of cordite filled the foyer while Sam picked himself off the floor. Sam felt a pain in his hip and grabbed at his side, his hand coming away bloody a second before Shaun opened the door. Sam lost control of his temper, setting his dark side free. Seeing Shaun kicking in the door, still holding the pistol and reloading, he crushed any remaining control of his temper. With a roar, Sam tackled Shaun, knocking them both back though the door and down the steps again. Shaun went down under the weight of the tackle, the gun flying out of his hand. Sam felt a jolt of pain in his left hip when they landed, but his rage was in control and he pushed the pain aside. He rained punches into Shaun's body knocking the wind out of him. While Shaun tried to cover his head, Sam climbed up on top of him, raining blows in his fury. Sam hit him harder with each punch, the image of Macy's battered face and body fueling his muscles. Shaun tried to fight back and landed a few punches on Sam but it only increased Sam's rage. Sam grabbed him by the neck and slammed Shaun's head into the ground a few times. When Shaun covered his head, Sam attacked his ribs until he felt the bones break. He felt pain in his knuckles and hands, smelled blood mixed with the dirt and the salt air, but couldn't stop his anger from consuming him. Sam heard voices, but they didn't register on his mind while he continued to beat Shaun. It wasn't until he was tackled by someone that he realized the yard was full of people. He saw blue lights everywhere and finally heard the officer tell him to stop struggling.

"Okay, okay, I'm done."

The officer handcuffed him and left him lying on the ground while he checked on Shaun. In the stillness of the moment, with his adrenaline fading, Sam felt the pain in his hip. He groaned trying to look down at the injury.

"He had a gun," Sam said loud enough for the officer to hear him. The man's demeanor changed in an instant.

"Who did and where is it?"

Sam shook his head. "I don't know where it went, but Shaun shot through the door and I think he shot me."

The officer shined the light on Shaun while he searched him and put zip tie cuffs on him. With the scene under control and two more officers to help, they found the gun. The ambulance arrived a few minutes later and took Shaun away first. The EMT put a bandage on Sam's hip informing him a second ambulance was on the way. Macy reached him a few minutes later. Sam's leg was throbbing and he was lying on the ground next to the front porch.

"Sam!" She shouted pushing her way through the cops to reach him. "Are you alright?"

Sam gritted his teeth. "I'm fine." She looked down and saw he was holding a large bandage over his hip. The bandage was soaked in blood.

"You're bleeding."

"Nothing life threatening, though a few inches to the left and…"

Macy was crying. "He shot you? He really shot you?"

"He was trying to get to you. I couldn't let that happen, now could I?"

The officer who tackled Sam came back to talk to him and ask him some questions until a second ambulance arrived. Despite her protests Macy was taken aside and questioned while Sam was checked out by emergency personnel for the second time.

She was allowed to ride to the medical center with him and follow him into the emergency room. Sam suffered through a couple of x-rays and an IV before the doctor arrived to see him.

"I'm Dr. Heath; looks like you've had an interesting night."

He showed them the x-rays pointing out the bullet lodged next to Sam's hip socket.

"Looks like we'll need to operate to remove the bullet. I'll have to see if there's any other damage once I get inside. Are you responsible for the other guy?"

Sam nodded. "How is he?"

"He'll live, but you did a number on him. He has six broken ribs, a broken jaw, broken nose, and a fractured eye socket. What did you hit him with, a baseball bat?"

Sam held up his scraped bloody knuckles. "These."

The doctor shook his head. "How much pain are you in? I can give you something for the pain until I can get the operating room ready."

Sam shook his head. "It's not bad. Can I have visitors?"

"Sure, I'll send her back so she'll leave my nurses alone," Dr. Heath said with a chuckle.

Macy arrived with the officer a few minutes later. She hugged him while the officer waited his turn at Sam.

"How are you feeling?" she asked.

"I'm fine, but the sawbones said he needs to take the bullet out, so I'm going to get cut on in a little while."

Sam looked at the officer. "Am I going to recover in the jail?"

"Mr. Richards, I just have a few questions for my report. Since Mr. Harrison has not regained consciousness to tell his side, we're holding off on charges. What was the cause of the disturbance?"

Sam took a deep breath and glanced at Macy. "A month ago, Mr. Harrison brutally beat his wife and nearly killed her. I was protecting her from him at my residence when he showed up and tried to push his way inside. After a short altercation at the door, he pulled out a revolver and I slammed the door. He fired into the door and I felt a sting in my hip. Before he could get inside again I tackled him and took the fight outside. You arrived at that point," Sam said.

The officer took some notes, and then looked up.

"How long have you known Mrs. Harrison? And what kind of relationship do you have with her?"

Sam smiled despite the pain in his hip. "I've known Mrs. Harrison for more than twenty years. We have a son together who was born before her marriage to Mr. Harrison." The officer nodded, taking down more notes.

"Have there been any encounters between you and Mr. Harrison before?" the officer asked.

Sam shook his head. "No, sir."

The officer closed his notebook when the doctor reentered the room followed by two nurses. "I have a surgical suite ready. We'll be taking you in shortly and it should be a few hours until you wake up. Any questions?"

Sam shook his head. "Can she stay until it's time to go back?"

Dr. Heath nodded slowly. "Sure," he said, leading the officer out of the room.

Macy leaned over and kissed him. "I'm so sorry. This is all my fault."

Sam reached up and touched her face.

"Listen to me, none of this is your fault. Shaun did this, not you. If I hadn't been there you could have been killed, which would have hurt me much more than a little gunshot wound."

"I should've said yes to you years ago when you asked me to marry you. Then none of this would have happened."

"We can't change what happened in the past. We can only look forward to what life offers and live in the moments we're given."

She held his hand until the doctor came in, then leaned over and kissed him.

"I'll see you in a little while," he said before they wheeled him out the room.

She watched him go and blew a kiss before he disappeared behind the door.

Sam woke from his surgery. The anesthesia made him groggy and it was hard for him to wake up. He sat still and focused on trying to take in his surroundings. Nurses came and went, stopping to ask him questions and checking his vitals. He was finally moved down the hall to a room where he went back to sleep. Daylight was coming through the window of his empty room when he woke. He was hungry and pressed the call button for the nurse. The woman came in a few moments later and after explaining what he wanted, she came back with some toast, coffee and the doctor. Dr. Heath checked his wound and nodded.

"Everything went well with the surgery, though the ball at the top of your thigh, where it connects to your hip, was chipped. I was able to extract the bullet but not the bone fragment. Because of the fragment, you may walk with a slight limp from now on." Dr. Heath reported. "I think you should relax here for a day or so, to let the healing start and make sure there's no infection. We should let you go by tomorrow afternoon if you cooperate."

"Don't worry; I don't want to stay any longer than I have to. Can I have visitors now?"

Dr. Heath smiled gently. "The young lady who was with you asked me to give you this when you woke up," he said, taking an envelope out of his pocket.

Sam thanked him for everything and waited until the doctor and the nurses were gone to open the envelope. Inside, he found a letter scribbled on hospital letterhead and stained with tears.

> *Sam, once again I'm writing a letter to tell you sad news. I'm returning to Raleigh tonight and I won't be here when you wake up. This stuff with Shaun and you is another example of why you should've moved on years ago and forgotten about me. I've brought nothing but pain and sadness in your life, yet you continue to love me. Why, I'll never understand. The best thing for you to do is stay away from me. While this is hard for me to say, and will be even harder to me to do, it's for the best. One day I might be worthy of your love, but right now I need time to heal, physically and emotionally. I know this will cause you more pain and for that, I'm sorry.*

> *I'll Love you always,*

> *Macy*

Sam put the letter back in the envelope and closed his eyes. He was sad and wished she was there. Once again, she was pushing him away after making him believe she wanted to be with him. He was in pain from his hip, but now it extended to his heart, depressing him and making him feel trapped in the room. Things were simple when he was out on the water. The storms he faced there could be sailed around or, with enough experience and courage, met head on in a battle of wills. The storms in his personal life were much harder for him to navigate, leaving him feeling lost in the tumult surrounding him. With her gone again, he knew what he needed to do. This time he wasn't coming back, there was nothing left for him on the mainland anymore and his soul ached for the warm breezes of the Caribbean. He would return to the one woman who was always there when he needed her: the sea.

Late in the afternoon, Lynn showed up with Mark. Sam asked Mark for some of his things from the house, which Mark was happy to get for him. When he and Lynn were alone, Sam showed her the letter. Lynn read it slowly, a look of disappointment spread across her face.

"I'm sorry Sam, Macy's stupid for doing this again. I don't know why you keep coming back when this is all you get from her."

"I love her. One day it'll work out."

"Either you're an eternal optimist or you have the worst case of denial I've ever seen. So, what are you gonna to do now?"

Sam thought for a minute. "I guess I'm going back to what I know best."

The next morning, the doctor came in to release him. Sam hobbled to Mark's car for the ride back to the house. He climbed the steps to the porch, where he and Shaun fought, walking with a cane and limping, which made him feel like a pirate. He spent the night in the room where he'd nursed Macy back from her depression and felt his own more acutely without her there beside him. Mark and Lynn stayed with him, despite his protests about being fine on his own. He was up early the next morning, the ache in his hip making it hard for him to sleep. He went downstairs and began cooking breakfast, which brought them down not long after. They found him late in the afternoon sitting in his room with a sea bag packed. He handed Lynn the key.

"The house is yours to use all you want, including Michael and Mark. I know they loved this house as much as Jack did, so come as often as you can. If I need it, I'll let you know a week ahead of time."

"You're giving up?"

"No, I'm just going back to visit the other lady in my life: the sea."

Seeing nothing was going to change his mind, Mark drove him to the airport in Kill Devil. Sam shouldered his bag and limped away from the car with a final wave goodbye. He waited until he was seated on his flight to Miami then ordered rum and coke, leaving North Carolina behind.

Chapter 10

The old man sailed out of Druif Bay in the pre-dawn light. The wind was up and pushed him along at over 20 knots. He looked at his charts and did some math in his head. He was a little over 2000 nautical miles from his destination and at his current rate, it would take four more days to make North Carolina. He'd slept, but only rested a little; dreams of his past haunting him like poltergeists whose spirits were doomed to never be at peace. He trimmed the sails to get the most speed out of them and sat back to relax for a while. He enjoyed his first cup of coffee and the sunrise. His mind seemed determined to make him relive the past on this trip. The long stretches of open water were good for contemplation and he was at the point in his life where he had started looking back at his legacy, wondering if he had made the right choices or what he may have done differently. His mind brought up another memory for him to explore while he sipped his coffee and examined his life.

Sam stood in front of the casket and felt hot tears run down his face. He felt a hand on his shoulder and turned to find a familiar face staring at him.

"Hey, Sam," the man said. Sam studied him for a second, and then realized who it was.

"John?" Sam asked. The man nodded and the two men hugged.

"I'm sorry, man. He was my best friend and I loved him like a brother." He looked down at the face of his best friend, Alex. John was Alex's younger brother.

"I know. He always said the best times of his life were with you."

"We sure had some good times together." Sam said with a forced smile.

John pointed to an older woman sitting by herself in a chair.

"I had to bring mom up here; she's getting to where she has a hard time driving."

"Excuse me," Sam said, walking over to where the woman sat. She saw him coming and stood, knowing who he was instantly.

"Sam, I knew you'd be here," she said, clinging to him for support. Mrs. Gina had always treated him like she treated Alex and it broke his heart to see her so upset. Standing in the foyer of the little church, the two grieved for their loss. Sam took a deep breath and removed a cloth handkerchief from his pocket, offering it to her. "Thank you, Sam," she said when John returned. "It's hard to believe he's gone. It doesn't seem real." Sam found her a chair and sat beside her, holding her shaking hands.

"I know, I always thought one day I'd move back here and build a house beside his where we could see each other every day. There's not much reason to come back to Ridgeland now," Sam said, wiping his eyes.

"I brought pictures of the two of you. They're over on the table," she told him after a moment of silence.

Sam helped her to the table and opened the book. There were pictures of Alex when he was in school, where they'd met each other. Sam turned the page and saw a picture of them in their baseball uniforms when they were eleven. Their faces showed the promise of a long life, filled with happiness.

"I remember you playing baseball together, there was no other combination as good at turning a double play," she whispered.

"I remember."

Sam relived his youth by looking through the pictures. Sam paused when he reached the pictures of them flying together. Seeing Alex's smiling face in the photos made him miss the man even more. Sam excused himself and walked outside. John followed him to where he stopped in the shade of an old oak tree.

"You alright?" John asked.

"No, not really."

"Why don't you come by the house tonight? There's a few things he wanted you to have. Maybe we can have a few beers and talk."

"Sounds good."

Sam stayed until visitation was over, and then headed for Alex's house, where John and Alex's mom, Gina, were staying. John invited him in and after sitting around talking for a while, Gina left to relax and unwind. John wandered into the kitchen and came back with a six pack of beer. He tossed one to Sam and they toasted Alex's memory.

"He always talked about the time you flew together. He always said it was the best time he ever had." John said.

Sam chuckled. "It was for me too. Did he ever mention the time we went to Vegas for the air race?" Sam asked. He then told John a story involving a naked woman, a parrot and being chased by two large bouncers. They were both laughing by the end. It was late and Sam was a little tipsy when he ambled into his motel room. He heard his cell phone ring.

"Hello?" he said when he answered, wondering who would call him so late.

"Sam, I just heard about Alex," Macy said. "Are you okay?"

It had been four years since he'd seen her last, right before going into surgery to remove a bullet from his hip.

"Macy? How'd you find out?"

There was a moment of quiet before she replied. "Jason called me. He thought you might need me."

Sam laughed out loud. "It would be better if I didn't need anyone, 'cause I keep losing everyone I love; it's a curse I'm learning to live with."

There was a long pause while she waited for him to continue. "I'm sorry about Alex. I know how much he meant to you."

Sam lay back on the bed in his room. "Thanks, sorry, but it's been a long day and tomorrow will be one of the hardest days I've had to go through in a long time. I should try to get some rest."

"I understand. I just wanted you to know I was thinking of you."

Sam bit back a smart remark. "Thanks."

She hung up without another word. Sam heard the click and killed his phone before tossing it on the bed beside him. He kicked his shoes off and, after dragging himself out of bed, hung up the suit he'd worn to the visitation. He didn't bother taking a shower, but rather collapsed into the bed and let sleep claim him.

The funeral was sad and Sam, dressed in his captain's uniform, helped carry Alex to his final resting place. At the end, he said goodbye to Gina and John, with the plan to go back to his room, pack and leave the mainland for the last time. He didn't feel like going back to Key West and work right now. He called Jason and told him he was taking some more time off.

Sam drove toward Savannah, not sure of his destination. When the car stopped, it was near the pier on Tybee Island. The sun was fading and the beach was nearly deserted. It was late May and a warm breeze was blowing along the beach. He walked while he thought about Alex and their lives. Alex had been a successful business man in the computer industry. He'd been married but didn't have children. His wife had been so distraught she'd been medicated through the service and couldn't even talk to Sam. Lost in thought, Sam walked aimlessly along the shore, alone with his memories. He finally turned to look back toward the pier and noticed he was a long way from his car. He started back toward the pier, when he spied a small ketch coming toward the beach. He watched the boat skim across the water, driven by the sea breeze. It looked a lot like the one Macy had first taken him out in long ago. It wasn't until it got closer that Sam noticed it was a woman was bringing it in. She dropped the sail and let the surf push the ketch up on the shore. Admiring the skill it took to land the craft, Sam decided to tell her how impressive the maneuver was. The sun was down below the horizon and it was getting dark. The woman heard him approaching, but continued to pull the boat up the beach to keep the tide from taking it. Sam stopped when she finally turned around.

Macy was even more surprised to see him than he was to see her. The years since the last time they'd seen each other, had been kinder to her than to him. Though they were both in their mid-fifties, Macy looked like she was in her thirties while Sam looked old. For a few moments, they stood facing each other, both having so much to say, but neither one finding the courage to speak.

"Sam, what are you doing on Tybee? I didn't expect to see you here."

"I was just clearing my mind. So, this is where you ended up? What made you come here?"

"Why don't you come up to the house and we can talk?"

Sam followed her up the dune to a house which seemed familiar. When he saw the pool and the house together, he stopped in his tracks.

"This is the same pool where we first kissed." he said, memories flooding over him, threatening to drown him. Macy laughed, not seeing the emotional strain on his face.

"Yep, you've got a good memory."

"It's about the only good thing left on me."

Macy led him past the pool and into the back door. She'd redecorated the inside and it was laid out different from what he remembered.

"Would you like some wine or beer?"

"Beer," he said, hoping it would dull the ache in his chest and stop the memories from bothering him.

She smiled, handing him a Corona and pouring herself a glass of wine.

"I was sorry to hear about Alex. I know how close you were, it couldn't have been easy for you."

Sam sipped at his beer. "He was one of those friends who I could just pick up with where we last talked. It was like we were never really apart."

She sat on the couch facing toward the beach. He sat a few seats away from her and looked at the view, watching the cargo ships waiting for the tide to rise, so they could make their way up the Savannah River. "You look good," she told him.

"I bet I look a lot better than the last time you saw me," he said, subconsciously adding sarcasm to the statement.

"Yes, you do," she replied, frowning.

Sam let the conversation lapse and took a long pull from his beer.

"I see you haven't forgiven me for leaving," she said after a few minutes of silence.

"You had your reasons. What are you doing now?" he asked to change the subject.

She set her glass down and focused on him. "I'm the lead biologist at Grays Reef Institute. It's nice to be out of the classroom and back in the research side of things again."

"As long as you're happy."

"I am happy," she said. "Shaun is locked away in prison and I'm past that part of my life. It's been a long four years, but I'm back on my own two feet again. My only wish is I had my family around me, including you."

Sam closed his eyes while she continued. "Being back here has brought back a lot of memories of good times. The first night we spent together was in this house. We first kissed in the pool out there and you first sailed right out there, off the beach. I realize now how stupid I was for pushing you away for so long. I want you, me, Jason and Sara to be a family. I want to be a part of my grand-children's life and not just someone they see once a year." Sam stood and walked toward the windows where he stood silently while his mind raced. *Now, after all she'd put him through, she wanted him?* He'd spent most of his life loving one woman who'd put everything else before him. Now, when they were older and her life was settled, she wanted him to be what he'd offered to be thirty years ago. The thought affected him differently than he'd expected. He'd made peace with the fact she'd never love him the way he loved her. Now she did, or thought she did. He thought he'd be happy to hear her finally say she wanted him to live out his days with her. But instead, he was angry at her for wasting so much of their lives.

"You're awfully quiet," she said when he didn't respond.

Sam turned around to face her and felt a twinge of pain in his hip. The pain focused his mind and reminded him of the last time he'd seen her, right before she'd left him while he was in surgery.

"Thanks for the beer, but I should be going. Take care of yourself," he said, opening the door and walking out before he could talk himself into taking her back. As he walked into the darkness he heard her calling to him from the porch. He didn't look back, but kept walking until he reached the car. Sam left Tybee with a heavier heart than when he'd arrived. He went to the airport and bought a ticket to Key West. He needed some time to fix his head again. While he was waiting for his flight he called his son.

"Jason, get both businesses together for a staff meeting tomorrow afternoon. I also want to see you and Sara at the sailboat first thing in the morning."

"Dad, is something wrong?" Sam hesitated for a moment.

"No, I just need to do something and I need you and Sara to help." Jason said he would see him the next morning as Sam heard his flight number being called. "Son, I have to go, my flight's boarding. I'll see you in the morning."

Sam arrived at his boat late that night and went straight to bed. He was up early and had breakfast with coffee prepared when Jason and Sara arrived. They sat down and noticed Sam was being quieter than usual.

"Dad, what's going on?" Jason asked when they were seated to eat.

Sam set down his coffee cup and looked at the two of them. "I'm stepping away from the business," he said, shocking both of them. "Jason, I'm handing over the cargo business to you. Sara, you're getting the cruise side. You may do with them whatever you like. Sell it all, run them, whatever you decide is fine with me. Just be happy."

Jason looked at him with concern. "Dad, you're scaring me. You aren't dying, are you?"

Sam chuckled. "No, and I don't mean to be so dramatic. I'm just ready for a change. I have more money than I could ever spend, but I work too much and I need a break. I'm going to take my boat and go sailing. I'll be checking in from time to time, and who knows when I might pull alongside one of the ships in port; but I need to get away and be alone for a while. So, what do you say?"

Jason looked at Sara. "If this is what you need, then okay."

"Thank you," Sam said, looking at Sara for her answer.

She sighed. "You know I'll do it if you ask. I'm just going to miss you. You've been more of a father to me than mine ever was."

She stood and hugged him. "There's one more thing I need to ask of you. Macy is missing out on Caleb's life. I know Angela would love to move back to North Carolina, so move the business headquarters there, so you can all be together."

Sam officially turned over control of the businesses to Sara and Jason in the staff meeting. He spent the rest of the week working on his sailboat, preparing it for a long journey. When he wasn't working on the boat, he was spending time with his grandson, Caleb. The night before he planned on leaving, Jason invited him over for dinner.

"When are you coming back, Pop?"

Sam kissed the boy on the head. "I'll try to get back soon. Maybe this summer we can take a trip together."

"Okay," he said, running off to play. Caleb was eight and loved being on the sailboat with Sam, pretending they were pirates. Sam was going to miss the boy and the time they spent together.

Angela hugged Sam. "I'm going to miss you. But I'm happy to be moving back home. You have to promise to take care of yourself. Sara and I won't be there to look out for you."

Sam smiled, glad his son had someone with such a big heart. "I promise, I'll try to behave."

Sam was surprised to see Jason sitting behind the wheel in the cockpit of the sailboat the following morning.

"Are you sure about this?" Jason asked. "What if I have a question about the business?"

"You can do this. I want you to know I'm extremely proud of you and Sara. You're everything I ever wanted you to be and more," Sam said, giving his son a hug. "I should be back before Caleb starts school in the fall."

Jason untied the mooring lines and Sam eased the boat away from the dock. He stopped long enough to wave at his son before putting his life behind him.

Chapter 11

The old man grinned while he raced across the swells. After all his time at sea, he still enjoyed the thrill of a down-wind run in a sleek craft. He took a moment to study the weather and saw a cold front on the horizon. He was making good time running along the Cuban coast. He'd planned to make the Turks and Caicos Islands but the flashes of lighting in the distance changed his mind. Checking his GPS, he noticed he wasn't far from Baracoa, a small port he'd visited many times through the years. He could anchor there in the harbor and not have to worry about the storm. The old man had been sailing for the last 18 hours and needed a break. Two hours later, he reached the sheltered port, dropped anchor, and readied the boat for the storm. The first rumbles of thunder rolled in the distance while he was below cooking supper. With nothing to do after eating, the old man went to sleep. Dreams of adventures and places he'd visited played like an old movie through his mind.

Sam was sitting at a cabana bar beside the beach in Rio de Janeiro. People covered the beach, playing on the sand and water. Sam held a cold beer and absently listened to a salsa band play through a worn speaker at a seaside vendor's shack. He'd been here about a month and found he liked Brazil. He wasn't fond of the city, but the countryside he found quite beautiful. He was watching a group of young women and men though his Ray Bans while they played volleyball on the beach. He felt a presence beside him and turned to find a beautiful woman sitting down, watching him with a slight smile on her face. She was wearing a knee-length tan dress, which hugged her curvy figure. Looking into her eyes, he was fascinated by her.

"Hola," she said sweetly.

Sam returned her smile, "Hi," he replied in English.

"Those girls are way too young for you," she said with a heavy Spanish accent.

Sam laughed at her abruptness. "What makes you think I'm interested in them? They're young enough to be my grandchildren."

She gave him a look of pity. "Because you're a man."

"So where should I be looking? At you perhaps?"

She laughed and fixed him with a smile. "Perhaps; you are visiting Rio?"

"I'm visiting now, but I've been here many times. My name is Sam; can I buy you a drink?"

"Shara," she replied before ordering something fruity and non-alcoholic. Sam signaled the bartender for another beer. He set the drinks down a moment later and Sam paid.

"You are staying here in the city?"

"I live on a boat. It's tied up in the marina. Have you ever been sailing?"

"No, though I love to watch the sailboats glide across the water."

"If you wish, I'd be happy to take you for a short trip."

She smiled but shook her head. "I don't know you well enough. Do you dance?"

"I know a little, but it's been a long time."

"If you're interested in getting to know me better, I'll be at my favorite dance hall tonight," she told him, writing down the address on a napkin and sliding it to him. "Come by and dance with me, maybe I'll consider your offer," she said, standing to leave. "Thank you for the drink."

He nodded politely and watched her walk away, admiring the view. He laughed at himself, picked up his beer and started walking down the beach toward the marina, whistling an old sea shanty.

The cab driver laughed when Sam told him the address. "You're going to dance all night Señor? I see you know how to win the hearts of Brazilian women."

"I'm just meeting a friend there," Sam said when they got underway.

The dance hall was old and looked run down from the outside. Sam wondered about going inside and getting robbed, but his driver assured him it was a good neighborhood. Sam could hear the band playing before he reached the door.

"I'll be back at midnight, unless you find somewhere else to stay," the driver said with a laugh.

Sam waved goodbye and walked inside. He found a place to sit and watch the dancers move around the floor. Sam ordered a local beer and watched the couples dance. He spotted Shara across the room and moved through the edge of the dance floor to where she sat. She watched him approach with an amused look on her face.

"Hola," he said, giving her a short bow.

"Welcome, these are my friends, Tia and Miola," she said, indicating the two women sitting with her.

Sam gave them both a smile. "Would you care to dance? I'll do my best to not step on your toes."

Her friends laughed, but Shara grinned and stood, offering him her hand. He led her to the dance floor. Sam put his arm around her, touching the small of her back lightly while he tried to remember the steps he'd learned in Honduras long ago. At the end of the song Shara was impressed.

"You're not as bad as you said."

"You're much better."

She laughed at the compliment. "You just need a little bit of instruction and you will be as good as any man in here."

"It would take a miracle worker."

Sam offered to dance with both of her friends between drinks. The band slowed down and he asked Shara to dance once again.

"So, did I pass your test?" he asked.

"The night isn't over yet. So, besides sailing and dancing, what do you do?"

"I retired from my business and I'm sailing where the wind takes me."

She was surprised. "You have no family?"

"I have a son who took over the business when I left and a grandson."

"No wife, or is she gone?"

"I've never married. There was a woman once, but that's a very long story."

She smiled. "The night is young; maybe you could tell me about it while you walk me home?"

Sam bowed his head slightly. "As you wish, m'lady."

Shara's apartment was a few blocks away and he gave her the short story of his relationship with Macy while they walked with her arm through his.

"What about you?" Sam asked. "I seem to be telling you more about myself than you're telling me."

"I'm not very interesting. I lived most of my life here in the city. I was married once, but he was killed in an accident long ago."

There was a quiet spell while they walked together, lost in memories from the past.

"When you're not dancing, what do you like to do for fun? Besides picking on men watching a game," he said with a laugh.

She failed to hide her smile at the question. "I like to read and one day, I'd like to travel, go see the world. What about you?"

"Well, it seems that we share a love for reading. I love music and I love to cook."

"I'm a terrible cook."

"Then perhaps you'll allow me to cook for you."

A smile crossed her face. "We will see."

They reached her apartment, neither of them ready for the night to end.

"Would you like to come up and wait for your cab?"

"Thank you, but I don't want your neighbors to talk," he said with a sly smile, making her giggle.

"Let the old hens cluck."

"Another time maybe?" he offered, kissing her hand. "Is there a way for me to reach you? I enjoyed your company and would like to return your hospitality."

She reached into her purse and wrote her number on a piece of paper. "You can call me tomorrow, if you wish."

She leaned close to him and kissed him lightly. "I look forward to hearing from you," she whispered before disappearing up the stairs.

Sam's cab arrived and took him back to his boat. He couldn't stop thinking about Shara. The next day, he wandered back to the same vendor on the beach, hoping she would appear, but he didn't see her. He called her late in the afternoon and they talked for over an hour. When he asked if she had plans for the night, he was disappointed to find she did.

"I'm sorry, but I have a friend's party to attend tonight. But I'm free tomorrow and don't have to work."

"Then what do you say to taking a short trip on the boat and dinner?"

She accepted and they set a time to meet.

"Bring a bathing suit with you in case you want to swim."

He spent the evening cleaning the boat, making sure it was in perfect shape. Shara arrived at noon, wearing a long sarong covering her bathing suit and carrying a beach bag on her shoulder. Sam helped her onboard and gave her a short tour.

"Make yourself at home. There are drinks in the fridge if you're thirsty."

She followed him back up on deck to watch him leave the marina. Sam cast off and used his motor to clear the harbor. Once he was free of traffic, he shut off the motor and raised the sails. Shara watched everything closely while he worked the boat.

"You're a good sailor," she told him.

Sam laughed. "I hope so; I've been doing this for nearly thirty years."

They sailed up the coast for an hour, dropping anchor near a small reef. They snorkeled around the reef and Sam speared a couple of fish for their dinner. They relaxed in the shade of the sails and sipped cocktails Shara made. Sam fixed sandwiches and sliced fresh fruit sprinkled with sugar, then filleted the fish and put it in a bag to marinate. Shara watched him and shook her head.

"How has no woman married you?"

"Because none would have me."

Shara frowned at the statement. "What about the one you mentioned before?"

Sam shook his head. "She turned me down and married another. I was even shot trying to protect her, but she still said no."

"Then she was a fool," she said fiercely.

Sam showed her how to set the sails while they drifted back toward the harbor and let her take the wheel. He docked the boat, and then went below to begin supper. Shara showered and changed clothes while he cooked. Sam brought out a small table and two teak folding chairs which he set up in the cockpit area. They dined on fish and grilled asparagus while they watched the moon rise, full and bright. Sam poured wine and asked her about her past.

"I grew up on a farm outside of the city until I was twelve. My mother and father sent me to a better high school in Rio and I learned to be on my own. After I graduated, I was married to Carlos, my sweetheart from school. He worked in the highway department as a surveyor. He was working on a project at the edge of the city when a drunk driver hit him. I was devastated and wanted to die myself. Through the help of my friends, I came out of my depression and started living again. I worked in the Foreign Trade Ministry as a secretary until I finally finished at the University. I was promoted and became the Human Resources Manager. I have been there long enough to retire, but I have nothing to retire for."

"What about your plans to travel?"

"I guess I've been putting it off because I don't want to go alone. My friends are happy here with their lives and don't want to leave, so I stay here and dream about traveling," she said, sipping her wine. "So now you know about me, what about your past?"

"Well, you know most of it from last night. I traveled all over the United States when I flew air shows and I've been all over the Caribbean and the Atlantic side of South America by sail. On this trip, I've been spending a little more time in each port than I did as a captain. It's been fun to play tourist, but I know what you mean about doing it alone. It isn't much fun without someone to share it with."

After dinner, Sam turned the radio to some soft Latin music. He and Shara danced under the stars, enjoying the music and the company. At the end of one song, Sam dipped her, ending with their faces close together. He leaned forward and kissed her, unable to restrain himself. To his surprise, she returned his kiss, pulling him closer. They missed the next song, because neither wanted to stop long enough to dance. When they parted, she took his hand and slowly led him to the salon. Sam followed her below and across the cabin to the door to his room. She stepped inside, releasing his hand long enough to reach behind her and unzip her dress. He started to ask if she was sure she wanted to do this, but she noticed and put her finger to his lips.

"Don't break the spell," she whispered, moving her finger to the buttons of his shirt. He kissed her while she removed his shirt, and then started on his pants. He gently removed her dress, neither of them rushing into what would come next. He kissed her neck while her hands ran across the muscles of his back. Kissing a spot behind her ear, he could hear her breathing harder. Her hand moved up his neck into his hair, gently running her fingers across his scalp. He picked her up and laid her on the bed, tracing his kisses across her throat to the same spot on the opposite side of her neck. He heard a slight moan escape her lips when he slowly ran his hand down her ribs, touching her with only his fingertips. Their first time together was tender and sweet with both wanting to please the other. After, they lay beside each other, listening to the sounds of the music and the water lapping against the hull.

"That was unexpected," he said at last, making her chuckle.

"It has been a long time; I'm surprised I remembered how. You're different from Carlos, more patient."

"It's been a long time for me, too. I understand what you mean, with Macy it was all rushed, not like with you."

She snuggled close to him and Sam could feel the heat of her body next to his. He wanted to ask if she would sail away with him, but he feared the answer she'd give. Closing his eyes and taking a deep breath, he decided to find out.

"Shara, would you like to go to Porte Allegra with me? I enjoy your company and would like to spend more time with you. I don't know where we're going with this, but I'd like to find out."

"I'd love to. I've never been there but I've heard it's beautiful," she told him excitedly. "Let me arrange for some time off and pack. When were you planning on leaving?"

"Whenever you're ready."

They spent a week on their trip to Porte Allegra. When they returned, she invited him to stay at her apartment and he accepted. Their lovemaking was becoming more frequent, as well as more passionate. The next morning, she found him in her kitchen, cooking eggs and wearing her pink bathrobe. Her laugh at the sight drew his attention from the eggs.

"Why don't you retire and sail off with me? Let's go see the world together," he asked, checking the eggs again. He held his breath, praying she'd say yes, but expecting her to treat him like Macy had.

She paused at first, thinking of all the reasons not too, and then remembered how much she enjoyed their trip to Porto Allegra and thought, why not? "I guess there's nothing to stop me is there? Is there room for two on your boat?"

Sam finishing the eggs and plated them, releasing the breath he'd been holding. "I think we'll manage."

Two days later, over dinner, she told him she'd turned her paperwork in and officially retired. "When can we leave?" she asked.

They spent a few days getting her affairs in order since they would be gone a long time. She moved most of her things into his room on the boat. Sam felt a youthfulness he couldn't explain while the two of them planned their trip. Shara spent hours each night looking at his charts and asking him about the places he'd been. Sam taught her about navigation and how to work the boat on small day trips and at night they would go dancing. She said goodbye to her friends at the end of the week and sailed off with Sam.

In the two weeks it took them to reach Trinidad, Sam decided she needed to meet his family. He called Jason and they talked a while about work for a few minutes.

"How is your trip going?" Jason asked him finally.

"It's going well. While I was down in Rio, I met someone who joined me on the trip."

Jason was quiet for a second. "Does this person happen to be a woman?"

"Yes, and I would like for you, Angela and Caleb to meet her. Can you meet me in Antigua this weekend?"

"Let me talk to Angela and see what's going on. I'll call you back in a few hours."

Sam hung up and went to work on dinner. Shara was cutting tomatoes for him and singing with the radio, when his phone rang.

"I can handle this," she said with a wink.

Sam walked up on deck to answer the call.

"Dad, we'll be there on Friday about noon. I have a condo rented for the weekend."

Jason gave him the address and Sam wrote it down.

"Great, I can't wait to see y'all."

"It'll be good to see you, too; we've been missing the warm breezes of the Caribbean. You know Mom moved up here near us, she asks me about you a lot."

"Tell her I said hello and I'm doing fine. How's Sara?"

"She's fine, though she misses you, too. She's another one who asks me about you a lot. You should call her and invite her, too."

"I may do that; it's been nearly a year since I've talked to her." Sam smelled the food from below and started down the stairs to help finish dinner. "I'll see you on Friday. Kiss Caleb and Angela for me."

"I will, see you soon, Dad," he said before hanging up.

Sam was in a good mood when he went below and told Shara the good news. She quizzed him over dinner about his family, asking him to show her pictures so she'd know them by sight. Later in the evening, Sam called Sara. She was excited to hear from him.

"Are you coming back? It hasn't been the same with you gone."

"I'm just passing through and after talking to Jason, I figured I'd call to check on you. Jason and his family are meeting me in Antigua this weekend to meet a friend of mine who's traveling with me. You should join us."

Sara was quiet and finally spoke. "It's a woman, isn't it?"

"It is, and she makes me happy."

"Does Macy know?"

"Only if Jason told her. I haven't talked to Macy in a long time."

Sara sounded sad when she spoke again. "I'd hoped the two of you would end up together one day. I'll be there; this woman must be something special to make you change your mind about Macy."

Sam was nervous when they reached the condo. He and Shara had a room of their own situated next to Jason's. They'd barely gotten settled when there was a knock on the door. Jason, Angela and Caleb were standing there and Caleb jumped into his grandfather's arms. "I missed you, Pop!" he said, squeezing Sam's neck.

Sam hugged the boy. "You must have grown a foot since the last time I saw you," Sam said, setting the boy down and turning to Angela. "Hello, honey," Sam said, hugging her. "You look prettier every time I see you."

"Thank you," she said with a grin.

Sam hugged his son, and then led them into the den where Shara was waiting.

"Shara Maltaz, this is my son Jason, his wife Angela, and my grandson Caleb. Everyone, this is Shara."

Jason smiled and held out his hand politely. Angela hugged her quickly. Caleb jumped into her arms and gave her a hug and a kiss on the cheek.

"You smell good," Caleb said with a grin. Shara beamed.

They sat on the couch and talked about their trip. Angela asked Shara about how she'd met Sam. She told them the story of them dancing and Angela laughed.

"I didn't know you could Salsa," she said to Sam.

"I learned a long time ago but I've gotten better thanks to Shara. She's a great teacher."

There was a knock at the door and Sam left to answer it. Caleb went with him and when Sam opened the door everyone could hear him shout, "Aunt Sara!"

Sam hugged her and led her into the room with the others where he introduced Shara.

"Shara, this is my partly adopted daughter, Sara Harrison. Sara and Jason are step-sister and -brother. Sara followed him down here when he started working for me and I hired her, too. She's been like a daughter to me and I gave her half of the business when I retired."

Sam went into the kitchen to get something to drink while Shara chatted with Sara. Angela came in a moment later and smiled at him. "I like her, Pop. Are you happy with her?"

Sam nodded. "It's good to have a woman around; she helps dull some of my sharper edges. What do you think Jason and Sara think of her?"

Angela studied him for a moment. "It really matters to you what they think?"

"It matters what all of you think. I know y'all may think it's fast, but I love her and I never thought I'd find someone at this point in my life. I'm getting older and I miss having a woman to love."

She pulled Sam into a hug. "I'm glad you did, but I'm afraid Jason and Sara are kind of stuck on you and their mom being together."

"I know and I'll always care for her, but she keeps putting other things between us and I can't wait for her forever."

"I think Jason understands, but he still holds onto hope. Don't worry; I'll explain it to him later."

They rejoined the group and Shara looked happy to see him return. Caleb wanted to go swimming so Angela and Shara volunteered to take him to the pool. Sam kissed Shara lightly before they left, then joined his family. Jason and Sara were sitting quietly when he walked in. Sam looked at them after he sat down.

"Alright, get it out of your system. Tell me what you really think."

Sara and Jason shared a look, then a laugh.

"I can't say that I hate her," Sara said grudgingly. "She's smart, polite and very beautiful. You obviously like her a lot, or you wouldn't have had us rush down here to meet her. So, what does it matter what we think?"

Sam looked at Jason who simply nodded in agreement. Sam looked at the two of them. "It matters because you're my family and I love you both. I also love Shara and I want to spend what's left of my life with her." He held up his hands to stop them from objecting. "I know you both dreamed of Macy and I getting married and living out our lives together. I held that hope myself for longer than either of you have been alive. But I've realized I'll never be as important to her as she is to me. With Shara, I have a chance to be happy in the years I have left. I'd be a fool to pass up this opportunity."

They were quiet while they thought about what he said. Jason finally looked at him. "Dad, if she makes you happy, then be happy. Like Sara said, she's beautiful, smart and adventurous; God knows you deserve someone like her. I'd still like to see you with mom, but I'm happy for you."

Sam looked at him gratefully. He looked at Sara and she sighed. "I'm trying to not like her, but I can't help seeing how happy you are with her. Jason's right, you deserve some happiness after all you've been through."

"Thank you both for understanding," he said, blinking away tears. "You're two of the most important people in my life and I wanted your blessing before I went any further."

They changed clothes and joined the rest of the family in the pool. Caleb and Sam played in the water with Sara and Jason while Shara and Angela sat together talking. Sara went to join them a few minutes later and left the boys together in the pool. After their swim, Sam took them all out to eat. After dinner, Sam and Shara kept Caleb for Jason and Angela to go out together. Caleb fell asleep leaning against Sam while he read the boy a story. Sam picked up the boy and carried him to the spare room. She followed and stood at the door watching while Sam put the boy to bed and tucked him in.

"You're good with him," she said in Spanish. "It's good to see a man who loves his family like you do." She'd learned on their first sailing trip that he could speak Spanish.

"Thank you, he's a good boy and I miss him," he replied in Spanish. "If it wasn't for his schooling, I'd have taken him with me."

"That would have been an interesting trip."

They went back into the den and she sat with her back against him and his arms around her. "You have a beautiful family. I like them."

Sam smiled and kissed her on the shoulder. "I'm glad you do, because I would like you to be a part of it."

She turned around and looked at him. "What're you saying?"

He reached into his pocket and pulled out a ring. "I'm saying, I'd like for you to be my wife."

She looked at him for a moment and then pulled him into a kiss. "Yes, I'd love to."

It was at lunch with his family the next day when they announced their engagement. Jason and Sara were happy for him, though he saw a little sadness in their eyes. They planned to be married in Brazil, on the beach. Angela and Shara were excited, discussing wedding plans for the rest of the visit. Caleb wanted to go with Sam and Shara when the weekend was over, but Sam talked him into staying with his parents. Jason had a few minutes alone with his dad on the morning they were to leave.

"Dad, are you sure about this? Getting married I mean. It seems like an impetuous move for you and that isn't your style."

Sam smiled at his son. "I know, but I can't help feeling this is right for me, Jason. I'll always love your mother, but I'm getting older. I've waited and been destroyed by her too many times. I have a woman who makes me happy and was willing to drop everything to be with me. That's something your mother refused to do more than once. I've lived like a hermit long enough. I'm ready to spend what time I have left with someone who loves me and shares my passions. Shara makes me better than I believe I can be."

Jason chuckled a little. "I understand; I feel the same about Angela. She absolutely loves Shara, by the way. I just want you to be happy and a little settled. Caleb misses you and talks about you all the time."

"I know, and I'll do better about being there for him," Sam promised.

They said goodbye in the lobby and Sara wished them both well.

"I hope you'll at least honeymoon with us," she told Sam when she hugged him goodbye.

He smiled. "If we don't, it will be our first vacation."

She smiled and hugged Shara before leaving with Angela, Caleb and Jason.

Sam and Shara were sailing for Key West when his satellite phone rang.

"Hello, Sam."

"Macy."

There was a long silence while he waited for her to speak.

"I talked to Sara a while ago and she said she and Jason had a nice little visit with you. Too bad that I didn't get my invite," she said, sounding a little hurt.

"I don't think you would've enjoyed it."

She chuckled a little. "So I've heard. I guess now, I know what it felt like when I showed up with Shaun, it really sucks."

"It does, but this wasn't about getting even. Macy, I waited most of my life for you, it's time I moved on."

"I wish you the best," she told him before she hung up.

Sam put the phone away and looked out across the waves. Shara came up from below and saw he was in a melancholy mood. She sat quietly with him watching the gulls floating on the breeze, until he turned and kissed her.

"What was that for?" she asked.

Sam smiled at her. "For being here and loving me."

Chapter 12

The old man was past the Bahamas and could see the lights of the Florida coast in the distance. He checked his position and decided to push on a few more hours. The weather was calm and the seas were somewhat quiet. The temperature was cooling off with the start of November and his hip ached from the chilly air. Opening the Thermos at his side and sipping some of the warm coffee helped ward off the cold for a while. He'd have to remember to put on more clothes before the next leg of the trip. Scanning the horizon for traffic, he spotted a freighter leaving Miami which would cross the bow before long. The old man was tired having been at the wheel for almost twenty hours. By the time he stopped to rest, it would be twenty-two hours straight he'd been on deck sailing.

"Not bad for a ninety-five-year-old," he croaked. The wind picked up a little, pushing the sailboat past the freighter without incident. The old man was bone tired when he finally reached the small marina. He docked the boat, securing everything, before limping downstairs for a shower. The hot water warmed him and after drying off, collapsed across the bed to sleep. He'd hoped he was too tired to dream, but it was only wishful thinking.

Sam was surrounded by his family. They had arrived in Rio the day before and were staying with him, but he didn't mind. With four bedrooms in the house there was plenty of room for everyone. The house sat on the side of a hill overlooking the sparkling turquoise ocean. Sam and Shara had lived there for fifteen years and built a considerable group of friends and neighbors who they once entertained regularly. Their home had become known for great parties, dancing and warmth shared with those around them. Caleb sat next to his grandfather, watching him silently, marveling at the strength of the man who'd suffered more than his fair share in life. Sam watched the waves on the ocean quietly, while Angela came in carrying a cup of hot coffee for him. Sam could smell the rich coffee he'd brought from Peru on the last trip he'd taken with Shara.

"Pop, here's something to help warm you up," she said softly.

Sam took the cup with a nod of thanks. He tried a smile but couldn't muster the energy. Behind him, Shara lay on their bed sleeping. Her breathing became shallow. Sam knew what it meant, his love was dying. They found a small mass four months before and had it checked. Their worst fears were realized when they were told she had inoperable cancer. Shara faced it bravely, refusing to take chemo so she could travel with Sam, but she was losing the fight. When her strength faded, Sam had done everything for her. In her last lucid moment, three days before, she'd held his hand and talked with him.

"I've had a good life with you. I'm thankful for the time we've had and my only regret is I didn't find you sooner. You have been a loving and kind husband, I couldn't ask for a more caring lover or friend. Always remember, I love you," she told him before drifting off to a painless sleep from her medication.

Sam looked into her dark brown eyes and kissed her gently before sleep claimed her. Her face softened and a smile crossed her lips.

"I love you too," he whispered.

The nurse Sam hired to live with them and help him take care of her, a young girl named Kali, had cried for hours after overhearing their last conversation. She was sitting in a chair by Shara's bed, wiping her eyes when she thought no one was looking. Sam turned away from the window and went to sit by Shara's side, displacing Kali, who went to stand near Caleb. Sam held Shara's hand, gently stroking her paper-thin skin. Her eyes were closed and she looked to be at peace. Angela was standing with Jason, sniffling while she watched them spending their last moments together. Sara stood at the foot of the bed trying to hold her emotions in check. Caleb was staying strong, but Sam could feel the tension in the young man and the rest of his family. He took his eyes off Shara long enough to look around at his loved ones. They were trying to be strong for him and it was comforting, but he needed a moment alone with Shara.

"Could you give us a moment?" he asked just above a whisper.

Kali checked her patient, and then turned, her hand brushing Caleb's when he hesitated to leave. Sam had seen them sharing glances across the small room. Caleb looked a lot like Sam, with dark eyes, hair, and skin tanned from hours in the sun, sailing with his grandparents. He'd lived with Sam since graduating from high school. He held a special place in his grandfather's heart, being his only grandchild.

"Go on, son. Kali will need you soon," he whispered to his grandson.

The boy looked surprised at the comment, but followed the woman, unwilling to see the pain in his grandfather's eyes. He held the door for Kali to exit, following her out. Once the door was closed and they were alone, Sam leaned close to his wife and kissed her lightly.

"It's alright for you to leave, my love; they're here to take care of me." He stroked her long silver hair tenderly. Light from the setting sun shone through the window and settled on her face, infusing her skin in a reddish glow. Sam heard her exhale and felt the muscles in her hand go limp. He waited for another breath, but it didn't come. Sam bowed his head and let the tears flow for his loss. Outside, the sun was covered by a cloud mirroring what he felt inside, all the light and warmth in his life was gone. He heard the door open sometime later and felt a hand on his shoulder.

"Pop, are you alright?" Caleb asked quietly.

"Ask Kali to come in please," Sam asked in a raspy voice.

Caleb noticed she was no longer breathing. He rushed from the room and seconds later, Kali raced in to check on her patient. She checked for a pulse and confirmed what Sam already knew, Shara was gone. She saw the tears in his eyes and ran from the room crying, followed by Caleb, who was torn between chasing her and staying with his grandfather. Sam felt all of his seventy-one long years when he stood. Jason, Angela and Sara had come to check on him and were standing at the door watching him through tears of their own.

"She isn't in pain anymore; she's at rest."

Angela rushed forward and hugged him while she cried. Sam patted her back and held her for a moment. Angela was more upset than he seemed to be, and Sam knew her heart was broken, she'd loved Shara nearly as much as he did. Jason hugged his father while Angela, left to check on Caleb.

"I'm sorry, Dad," Jason said sadly.

"I know, thank you son."

Kali retuned with Caleb a few minutes later. Sam noticed them holding hands when they walked in and smiled inwardly. When Shara first met Kali, she had regaled her with stories about her grandson and how handsome he was. Kali had been polite but it seemed she'd listened to her patient more than Sam imagined. Shara was a crafty woman and it appeared her matchmaking skills had born fruit. Sam walked onto the balcony and watched the lights of the city below, when the paramedics arrived. He stayed there until they were gone. Sam knew he couldn't handle watching them take her away from him, so he stood, looking out at the sea, waiting, while they completed their grisly task. He heard someone talking around the corner of the wraparound balcony that connected the bedrooms from the outside. Kali had taken up residence in the room next to the one Sam shared with Shara. He quietly shuffled to the corner and peeked around to see if Kali was alright. Caleb and Kali were standing on the balcony and she was crying on his shoulder.

"She was a beautiful woman with a good soul," Kali told him.

"She was always fun to be around. She was a great dancer, too."

Kali looked at him in surprise. "She danced?"

Caleb laughed at a private memory of his grandmother. "My Pop made me dance with her when I was young and would visit. She taught me how to Salsa downstairs in the living room. She and Pop loved to dance together. There was a place down in the city where they would go to dance sometimes, getting home late in the night. They would come home exhausted but smiling."

"I wonder what he'll do without her," Kali mused. Caleb rubbed her back gently.

"Pop's a lot tougher than people think. He used to tell me that he'd survived hurricanes, heartache and his own hardheadedness more times than a duck has feathers," Caleb said, mimicking Sam's voice. "I figure he'll head to sea again. Dad says the salt water is like a salve for Pop's soul. Every time life hurts him, he heads back to the ocean to heal."

Kali sighed. "I guess that means you'll go with him?"

"I can't let him go alone. I don't want anything to happen to him."

"I know, I couldn't bear to lose him either. He's been like a grandfather to me."

Sam felt like a voyeur listening to their private conversation. He left them and went back to look at the ocean. A few minutes later, Sara came out to check on him.

"I'm sorry, Sam; I know how much you loved her." She hugged him and he put his arm around her shoulders.

"Thank you, honey. She's better off where she is. Knowing that brings me comfort," he said. "Are they done inside?"

"They are; some of the neighbors arrived and wanted to speak with you."

Sam wiped his eyes and stood up straight. Sara watched him, amazed at the change in him.

"How can you face anyone right now? You've got to be about to collapse."

"Because Shara and I lived every day like it might be our last, once she found out about the cancer. I've had months to prepare myself for this day. It isn't easy, but what in my life has been?"

Sam spent the evening accepting condolences from his neighbors and friends. Stories were shared about the two of them and memories flowed between those who came by, assuring Sam that Shara would never be forgotten. He grew weary, but refused to rest until everyone was gone. He looked at the bed he'd shared with her and couldn't bring himself to lie in it without her. He walked onto the balcony and stretched out in a chair, covering himself with blankets. Kali found him there the next morning and shook him gently to wake him.

"You'll catch pneumonia out here. You should be in bed," she said, once he was awake.

"I'm fine, I've slept under the stars most of my life. I couldn't sleep in there without her in the room." Kali gave him a look of pity and sorrow.

"You're going to have to sometime. I'm going to miss being here; you've been so good to me. It feels like home."

Sam smiled at her. "You don't have to be in a hurry; this is a big house and without enough people around, it gets lonely. That's why Shara and I used to host so many parties."

She returned his smile. "I heard stories last night from your friends. Everyone spoke of the parties with a twinkle in their eyes. They said you and Shara were excellent hosts and no one left until early in the morning."

Sam smiled. "It's been a long time since we've had a party here. I'm afraid the tradition may come to an end. Regardless, you don't have to leave right now. You've been a great help to me and to Shara, thank you, for taking such good care of her."

Kali was touched and she kissed him on the cheek. She left him to get dressed. He had arrangements to make and things to do.

The funeral was melancholy and by the end of the service Sam was spent. Kali was worried he was pushing himself too hard. When he returned home, Sam went to his room and lay down. Angela and Kali fussed over him until he shooed them from the room. He slept through dinner and breakfast the next day. When he finally emerged, he felt better than he had in months. The sun was shining and he felt the pull of the tide on his soul. He managed to sneak away from his family and drive down to his sailboat. The motor was running and he was untying the lines when Caleb and Kali showed up.

"Nice try, Pop," Caleb told him. "You aren't as sly as you think. I figured you'd make a break for the boat soon. You aren't going anywhere without me."

Sam looked at them and noticed they had their arms around each other, he smiled and relented.

"Alright then," he said. "How about I take you two out for a short ride?"

"I've never been sailing!" Kali exclaimed, making Sam smile wide.

"Then it's a good time to try it. Caleb, cast off the bowline, the tide is running from us."

They slid out of the harbor and Sam hoisted the sail. He felt the familiar first push of the wind in the sail and the freedom it offered. They ran north on the breeze and Sam let Caleb sail the boat while he went below and made lunch. He returned and handed them plates with avocado sandwiches and fruit. He sailed while they ate and sipped at the wine he'd poured for them. He found the place he wanted and dropped the sails and anchor, pulled out two fishing rods and cast them off the stern. Caleb couldn't help but laugh at him. They caught several fish with Kali catching the biggest. Sam took the fish below and had Caleb start them toward home. Sam prepared the fish and by the time they were docked, everything was ready. Sam called them down to the cabin where two plates under candlelight awaited them.

"Thank you for sharing today with me. What we did today was the same thing Shara and I did on our first date. We fished in the same spot we visited today and when we returned, I fixed her the same meal I've prepared for you," he said with a mixture of sadness and pride. "It was also the first night we spent together and the night I knew I was in love with her," he confessed. He poured wine into two glasses. "I'll wish you a good night now," he said, turning to leave.

Caleb got up and caught him at the steps to the cockpit. "Pop, please join us."

Sam looked at his grandson and smiled slyly. "Three's a crowd son, and don't think for a moment I didn't set all this up today. I might be old, but there's more than one trick still up my sleeves," he told him with a wink. Sam left him standing there and walked up the dock. For the first time in weeks he smiled and began whistling a sea shanty he remembered.

Jason and Angela were waiting for him when he walked in.

"Where have you been, and where's Caleb?" Jason asked. "We haven't seen you, him or Kali all day."

Sam looked at his son and chuckled. "He's quite safe and hopefully doing as well as I did once upon a time. He, Kali and I went on a little day trip on the boat. I left them there, having dinner and some wine."

Angela stifled a giggle, but Jason shook his head.

"Dad, we were worried about you. When the boat was gone we thought you'd taken off again."

Sam looked at his son and put his hands on Jason's shoulders. "I've never left without talking to you first. I might leave again, but it'll never be without telling you."

Jason wasn't happy, but Angela understood.

"Honey, Sam's fine and Caleb is on a date. I think we can relax now. I'm sure Pop's hungry, so why don't you and Sara get him something to eat?"

"Okay," he said, heading for the kitchen.

Angela looked at her father-in-law and laughed. "You're a sneaky old man. So, how'd your matchmaking go?"

Sam faked an innocent look. "I don't know what you're talking about," he said with a smile.

Angela laughed. "So how did you do it?"

"I knew Caleb would figure I'd try for the boat at some point. I knew he and Kali were out together on an errand. He's a smart boy and as suspicious as his mother about me. All I had to do was wait at the boat for him to show up with her and the trap was set. I took them to the same place Shara and I went on our first date and I fixed them dinner on the way back. In essence, I recreated my date with Shara, using them as stand-ins."

Angela was speechless.

"I explained it to them before I left."

She shook her head. "You're even worse than I thought at being sneaky," she said laughing. "I'll have to keep a better eye on you."

Caleb showed up with Kali the next day around lunch time. Sam was curious about their night but resisted the urge to pry. Angela was less subtle about it and cornered her son later to ask. Kali was helping Sam get rid of Shara's medicine when Caleb came in. Sam caught the look in her eyes when she looked at his grandson. He smiled to himself.

"Kali, could you give me a minute with Pop?" he asked her sweetly.

She smiled and kissed him on her way out.

"You're a sneaky old thing," Caleb said when she was gone. "And I love you for it."

"So, last night went well?"

"Yes" he answered, his face turning a little pink.

Sam laughed out loud.

"It's been a long time since I've heard you laugh, I've missed it."

"I know, but I'm glad you and Kali are getting along so well. Maybe we could all have dinner tonight, unless the two of you have plans?"

Caleb shook his head. "You're incredible. When you put it that way, I guess I have to accept."

After dinner, Sam put on a record and looked at Angela.

"Care to dance?" he asked while the Salsa band played.

Angela laughed and took his hand. He spun her around the floor in the huge den for a while, until Jason cut in. Sam went over to Kali and held out his hand.

"What do you say, my dear?"

She smiled and stood up to dance with him. Caleb cut in a few minutes later and Sam watched two generations of his family dancing across the floor of his den. They danced for over an hour before Sam excused himself and limped upstairs to his room. He showered and lay in the bed listening to the music play. Tears filled his eyes when the song he'd first danced to with Shara played. He sang in Spanish with the song until sleep overpowered him.

Inevitably, Jason, Sara and Angela tried to get him to return to the States with them. Sam shook his head, slowly.

"I live here now."

"At least come and visit," Sara told him. "I'm sure you could use some time away from here."

"Maybe one day, but not now. How's your mother doing?" he asked Sara.

She laughed. "She lives next to us and Jason visits with her every day. She's been asking about you and wondering how you were doing."

Sam was quiet for a moment. "I haven't talked to her in years, but Caleb would keep me informed of how she was doing. Shara knew about it and would only laugh. She told me that when she was gone, at least I would still have someone in this world who loved me like she did," he said, his voice cracking. He took a deep breath and smiled. "You know, Sara, I have known and loved some unique and amazing women in my life. Shara, Macy, you and Angela, you're all special to me."

Sara hugged him. "You're special to us too. You're the glue that holds us together."

Chapter 13

The old man was making good time. He'd left Cape Canaveral after ten hours of rest and was off the coast of Jacksonville. The farther north he went the colder it got. The sun was up and warming the air a little, but he was still chilled. He considered lowering the sails and going below to grab a jacket, but decided against it. The wind shifted, making the canvas luff and taking the wind out of the large Spinnaker he had raised. Using the controls in the cockpit, he dropped the sail and adjusted the sheets. When he was done, he set the autopilot and clipped onto the safety, going forward to gather the Spinnaker and stow it in the sail locker. He returned to the cockpit feeling tired from his labors. His back and shoulder hurt, along with his left arm. *You're showing your age, old man*, he told himself, settling into his place again and checking the line of clouds gathering over Florida to the west. He glanced at his chart and checked his GPS to get a position fix. He did some quick math in his head and figured he was about three hours away from his destination. With nothing else to do but dodge the local sea traffic, the old man went back to thinking about his life.

Sam stood on the deck of the *Carolina* with a large crowd gathered in front of him. Standing at the forefront of the crowd, were two young people he cared for a great deal. Captain Marko Wade and Sara Harrison stood there staring at each other while he performed their wedding ceremony. Doug Stephens stood next to Marko as his best man, while Angela stood beside Sara as her Maid of Honor.

"By the power vested in me, as Captain of this vessel, I pronounce you husband and wife," Sam said to the assembled crowd. "I'm proud to present Captain and Mrs. Marko Wade. Captain, you may kiss your bride," Sam told him with a wink.

The crew and friends, gathered for the ceremony, cheered while they kissed and turned to face the assembly. Sam joined in the cheers with the rest of the *Carolina*'s crew, his gaze drifting to where Macy stood clapping for her daughter and new son-in-law. Her hair was cut short and had turned grey like his. However, where he looked his seventy-five years; she looked much younger. The years of sun and salt, had sapped the youth from his skin, youth she still enjoyed. She glanced at him when he stepped forward and led the couple down the aisle, to the steps leading below deck. With a few seconds alone with the happy couple, Sam turned and congratulated them both.

Sara hugged him. "Thank you for coming to do this. It means so much to us."

Marko shook his hand. "She's not kidding. I wouldn't have anyone else marry us, Captain."

"I wish for you to share a lifetime of happiness with each other. It was my pleasure to do this for you. I only have one request, a dance with the bride," he told Marko.

Sara laughed and Marko nodded. "Of course."

Sam slipped away and went back on deck. He went to his spot on the stern where he used to watch the stars during the night watch.

"Hello, stranger," Macy said from behind him. "You're a hard man to find."

Sam grunted, and then turned around.

"I wasn't trying to be, I was just taking a minute to visit with an old friend."

She looked around at the empty space around him. "There's no one here."

Sam smiled, turning back to the rail.

"I'm talking about the ship. I spent many watches standing here looking at the sky and telling my dreams to the ship. She's a great listener."

Macy remained silent while he rubbed the wooden railing affectionately.

"How have you been?" she asked him. "Caleb says you don't entertain like you once did."

Sam turned around and looked at her. There was sadness in her green eyes, but he didn't know if it was because of him or something else.

"No, I don't," he said sadly. "I leave that to Caleb and Kali now. My entertaining is done around a cup with the other old men in the local coffee shop. I haven't felt the need to entertain much since Shara passed."

She saw the emotion in his eyes for an instant before he shut it away. His wife's death had changed Sam, it made him seem less of the legend his crews believed him to be and made him seem tragically human.

"How's life at the beach?" he asked to change the subject. She walked over to where he stood and stopped beside him. She looked out at the water of Botany Bay.

"It's nice, but lonely. Since I've retired, I have a lot of time on my hands, but little to actually do. The only thing I enjoy anymore is kayaking along the creeks near the house."

Sam smiled. Jason found them before they could continue. "Sara is looking for both of you for a picture."

Sam nodded, hesitating a few seconds while Macy walked away with their son. Sam looked out at the turquoise water and then up at the cloudless sky. *I should have stayed in Rio*, he thought.

He didn't want to keep Sara waiting and he found them at the ship's wheel. The photographer positioned everyone and took several pictures. The real party began after the pictures were done. A band played while drinks and food were served by the crew. Sam sat at a table watching Caleb and his new wife, Kali, dance together. The boy lived with him in Brazil and was becoming more Brazilian than American. Sam picked at his food and sipped on Argentinean wine he'd brought for the wedding. He danced in place of the bride's father while Marko danced with his mother.

"You are a beautiful bride. I wish you and Marko all the happiness in the world."

Sara smiled at him. "I am happy. Are you alright? You've been kind of quiet today."

Sam smiled at her gently. "I'm fine. I just don't want to steal the spotlight from you and Marko."

Sara laughed. "Sam, I could never thank you enough for all you've done for me. You took in a girl you should have hated, and treated her like a daughter. Then you gave me half of your company and set me on a course leading to Marko. You have to be the most generous person I've ever met."

"I could never have hated you. You proved your worth to me and Paradise Shipping more times than I could count, that's why I gave you the company. After meeting and being around your father, I knew you needed something different in your life. You flourished under the pressure of running a business and I'm very proud of you."

Sam kissed the top of her hand when they finished their dance. During the next slow song, he danced with Angela and danced a Salsa with Kali. Afterwards he relaxed and recovered. Macy found her way over to his table and sat beside him.

"Sara seems happy; I guess you played a large role in that. Thank you."

"All I did was spot a talented young woman and gave her a chance," Sam responded.

"Would you have noticed her if she hadn't been my step daughter?"

Sam shrugged.

"You set both of my children up with a career and you're doing the same with our grandson. I wish he'd followed in my footsteps rather than yours, but you've always had a way of drawing people to you."

Sam remained silent, sipping his wine. The music changed and the band played a slow song.

"It's been a long time since I've danced with you. Do you mind a dance for old times' sake?"

Sam stood and held out his hand to her. He swayed to the music with her, on the deck of the ship where he'd dreamed of holding her for so long.

"This brings back a lot of memories," she said with a sad smile. Sam didn't meet her eyes.

"I know, but memories are all they are. I made a promise to myself that I wouldn't look back anymore. I only live in the moment, in case it's my last."

"I guess that's not such a bad way to live. I think about the past a lot. I can see clearly now what I couldn't see then. I know now how much I hurt you over the years. I'm sorry for the pain I've caused you."

Sam looked at her. "I'm not," he replied, surprising her. "Because if things had worked out with us, then I wouldn't have met Shara."

Macy was surprised at his response. "You really did love her, didn't you?"

Sam nodded. "The years we shared together, were worth the pain of losing her."

Macy looked away from his eyes. "I wish someone loved me like that," she said without thinking.

Sam stopped in his tracks and looked at her. "Someone did," he said before turning and walking away, leaving her standing alone on the deck.

He found Sara and Marko and wished them well before heading for his room and locking the door behind him. Caleb came to check on him later and Sam told him he was just tired. Sam heard a knock on his door a little later and a familiar voice came through the door.

"Open up, you old pirate," Doug Stevens said from the other side.

Sam opened the door letting his old friend in. Doug held a full bottle of wine and two glasses.

"I need a drinking partner," Doug said, stepping inside.

Sam looked at his former First Mate. "Why me?"

Doug looked at him and grunted. "Because I know you better than anyone else in the world. I saw you leave Macy on the dance floor and I know the sight of heartbreak on your face caused by her," he told Sam, pouring the glasses full and holding one out to him. "I was there for all of it, remember?" Doug asked.

Sam took the glass and nodded. "I remember, though I've tried very hard to forget."

"Did she turn you down again? Or has she found another one to take your place?"

Sam shook his head. "No, it was a comment she made."

There was a knock at the door and they heard Macy's voice from the other side.

"Sam, I want to speak with you. I know you're in there, I've checked everywhere else."

Sam looked at Doug, who pointed at the bed and then to the bottle. Sam understood what he was saying and laid down facing away from the door. Doug waited a moment, and then opened the door slightly.

"Hello Macy. I'm afraid you're a little late. Sam passed out a moment ago. We've been drinking and reminiscing."

Macy pushed past him and looked at Sam lying in the bed. She saw the glasses and the bottle on the side table and let out a sigh.

"Great," she said sadly. She picked up the glass and drained half of it. "I think he has the right idea. Just drink until you don't feel anymore and act like nothing ever happened."

"Macy, he has every right to drink as much as he wants, for whatever reason he chooses," Doug said, turning angry. "If I were him I would've been a fall down drunk a long time ago. He just continues to pick himself up and fight despite how many times life knocks him to the mat. He once laughed and told me that he was the reincarnation of Odysseus, doomed to never find rest on land. I laughed at him then, but he was more right than I could've guessed."

Macy stared at Doug venomously. "I love him, I always have, despite what you or anyone else thinks."

"Do you?" Doug asked her matching her intensity. "Because every time he tried to get you to be with him, you had a reason not to. It sounds like you're more in love with the idea of him than the man himself. I watched you break his heart over and over again but I never saw him waver in his love for you. Hell, he still loves you enough for you to hurt him, despite loving another. Go away and leave him alone, the man's suffered enough."

Sam was about to turn and tell Doug he was being too harsh on her, but his friend's words rang true. Sam looked back at his life and saw it clearly for the first time.

"I won't bother him anymore. I came here to tell him I would go with him anywhere now, but obviously his friends hate me enough to sabotage it for us. I won't make him chose between me and you, because I'm not sure he wouldn't choose you. I'm leaving tonight and he'll never hear from me again. Tell him or don't when he wakes up. I don't care what you do," she said before storming out, slamming the door behind her.

Sam waited a few moments before sitting up and looking at Doug.

"I'm sorry, Sam. I've been waiting a long time to get that off my chest."

"No apologies necessary, women are easy to find; good friends are much harder."

"There's still a half full bottle of wine left," Doug said with a grin. "Tell me how you found this stuff."

Sam laughed while he refilled his glass then Doug's. "It was on a trip I took with Shara to Argentina," he said, beginning the story.

Sam woke the next morning with a headache, still wearing most of his clothes from the wedding. He showered and put on civilian clothes before heading out in search of food. He saw Doug sitting at a table and swerved to join him. Doug kicked out a chair for him.

"Drop anchor old buddy, you look like hell," Doug said with a grin.

Sam fell into the chair a moment before one of the crew came by to ask what he wanted for breakfast.

"Pancakes, syrup and coffee, black."

Jason appeared at the door, looked around for a second, then bee-lined for the two men. Sam could tell he was annoyed, watching Jason's face while he walked toward them.

"What happened with you and Mom?" he asked walking up to the table. "She left the ship last night and said she was going back to North Carolina."

Sam was about to answer when Doug intervened again.

"It's considered rude to ask about the relationship between a man and a woman. You were raised better."

Jason turned his anger on Doug.

"Doug, I'm not sixteen anymore and you're not dad's First Mate. I asked him a question and I deserve an answer. It's also considered rude to stick your nose into other people's business."

Sam cleared his throat. "Like you're doing?"

Jason smirked at his father. "Touché, but since you seem to agree I'm just being rude this morning, my question stands."

Sam waited until he had tasted the coffee a crewman brought him, before answering his son.

"I don't know why she left," Sam explained. "She came by my room last night when Doug and I were drinking and talking about old times. I'm sure something was said that hurt her feelings, but I can't remember what it was."

Jason looked at Doug, who held up his hands. "I don't remember anything."

Jason shook his head. "I have to make sure she got home safe, excuse me," Jason said, stomping off in a foul mood.

"One day he'll understand," Doug said.

"I hope not. Because I wouldn't wish my life on anyone, especially my own son."

Sara and Marko were on their honeymoon and the *Carolina* was due to sail in a few hours. In a moment of insanity, Sam and Doug decided to race to the top of the mainmast while the crew cheered and placed bets on them. Sam beat his old friend by a step and laughed.

"You still climb like a monkey up those lines," Doug told him. "But you're getting slower."

Jason walked over to them and shook his head. He had cooled off and apologized for how he had acted.

"You two old men are crazy. I hate to say this, but it is time to go, unless you want to join the crew."

Sam and Doug shared a laugh. "I'm sure we could teach these kids all kinds of interesting things," Doug said with an evil grin.

"That we could, but why corrupt these young, saintly sailors," he joked when some of the crew passed them.

Sam and Doug said goodbye at the beach where the long boat dropped them to catch their flights home.

"Why don't you come down and visit me in Brazil?" Sam asked. "I have plenty of room and it wouldn't cost you anything but the ticket."

"I might, but right now I have to get back to work. I have a sailing team to coach back in Miami. You take care of yourself, you old pirate."

It was a month later when he received a letter in the mail from Macy.

Sam,

This is the last letter you will get from me. I have been thinking of us a lot recently and I see now you have every right to not want to speak to me. For the sake of Jason and Caleb, please remember me fondly, if they ever ask about us. I know saying I'm sorry couldn't begin to cover how much I've hurt you over the years, but I'm truly sorry. I had hoped one day we could be together, but I see now it was a dream that will never come to pass. I wish you the best and hope you can find it in your heart to forgive me. If you do, I'm never more than a call or letter away from running away with you.

With all my love,

Macy

Sam read the note three times before putting it back into the envelope and looking across the ocean. He tried to decide if he should write back to her or not. He was still thinking when Kali found him sitting out on the balcony off of his room. She spotted the letter and noticed the address. She and Caleb had heard through the family grapevine, something had happened between Sam and Macy at the wedding, but neither of them asked, out of respect for Sam's privacy.

"You alright?" Kali asked, drawing his attention.

"I'm fine, dear. I've just been sitting here thinking."

"Is it anything I can help with?"

"No, I'm just wrestling with a decision."

She sat next to him on the balcony, looking over the city below.

"Pop, you've mourned long enough. It's time you lived again. I've heard stories about the entertaining you once did here and how much fun it was. Your friends from the neighborhood miss you and pray you will once again spread the happiness you once did."

Sam looked at her for a long moment and she felt bad for having scolded him. He turned his head and looked back at the scene in front of him.

"Perhaps you're right and we should have a grand party like we used to. In fact, I would like you to help me plan one. Parties are better with a woman's touch," he said, warming to the idea. "It's time I rejoined the community I enjoy so much."

Kali was excited. "Pop, this will be an amazing party. I can't wait to tell Caleb."

She hugged him and headed downstairs to tell her husband about the party. Sam picked up the letter and made his decision. He put the letter next to his bed, then picked up a notebook and a pen, then began to write.

Macy,

I'm sorry for the way I acted. I've been having a hard time recovering since I lost Shara and it has dreadfully affected my moods. There is no reason for you to apologize to me for the past. What happened is over and gone. I want you to know I don't harbor ill feelings for you and my memories of us are only good ones. If you should ever need me I'll be there; you have only to send word and I'll come.

Yours always,

Sam

He sent the message with the mail the next morning, on his way to the coffee shop to join his friends from the community for a muffin and coffee. He poured himself into planning the party and getting everything ready. The night of the party, he was a lively and energetic host to the people of the neighborhood. Caleb and Kali were amazed at the transformation in him.

"Pop, I don't know what changed your mind, but it's good to see you like this again."

Sam had only smiled as he looked at the boy. "It's been long overdue. You have your wife to thank for my change. Take special care of her and tell her how you feel about her every chance you get."

Caleb looked at his grandfather with sudden concern.

"Are you alright? You sound as if you are about to leave."

Sam shook his head. "Not right now. You can't get rid of me that easily. It's just something I should have told you long ago."

Chapter 14

The old man was nearing the Hatteras inlet and was forced to focus on the traffic moving through the cut. He was seven miles from his destination according to his GPS. His body was tired and battered but he'd done what he started out to do; what he promised he would do. He spotted the dock he was looking for off Sandy Bay and checked the wind and the tide while he made his approach. He dropped the mainsail and the jib when he got close and let the wind and tide bring him to the dock. Two men waited on the dock watching his approach and stood by to catch the dock ropes. He tossed the rear line then limped forward to toss the bowline, pushing the bumpers over the side as he went. When the boat was tied off, he packed the sails into the canvas and finally stepped off onto the weathered wooden dock.

"Hey, Dad," Jason said hugging his father.

Sam embraced his son. "How's your mother?"

Jason released him and let out a sigh. "She isn't doing very well, but she'll be glad to see you."

Sam turned to the other man on the dock and smiled.

"Hello, Marko, good to see you again." Marko shook his hand, returning his smile.

"You, too, Captain. I see you've kept up your skills," he said, using his head to motion toward the sailboat.

"It's like walking, you never forget."

Jason and Marko led him up to the house he knew so well. He saw touches of Macy's style everywhere on the house. Kali, Caleb, and Angela, greeted him at the door. Sam hugged each of them, taking a moment to say hello. Kali and Angela were crying softly and he feared he'd arrived too late.

"Where is she?" he asked Angela.

She pointed upstairs and Sam walked to the staircase, starting a long, slow climb to the top. He had to take a break to catch his breath, but only stopped for a few seconds. He knew where to find her; she would be in the master suite. He walked to the open door, finding Sara sitting next to her step mother, wiping her eyes and holding Macy's hand. Macy lay on the edge of the king-sized bed with her eyes closed. He paused at the door and watched for a moment. He could see the rise and fall of Macy's chest and knew he'd made it in time. He stepped inside and touched Sara's shoulder. She looked up at him and jumped out of her seat.

"She's been asking for you. I'm so glad you're here at last," Sara said hugging him.

Sam patted her on the back while he studied Macy. Her breathing was shallow, reminding him of Shara's last moments.

"I made it," he said, pushing aside the bad memories.

Macy's eyes fluttered, and then opened. He released Sara and she stepped aside while Sam moved to Macy's side.

"Hello, Macy," he said with a smile. She looked at him for a long moment before she reached out and he took her hand.

"You're really here? I've dreamed of you being here so many times; I had to make sure I wasn't dreaming again."

He sat down heavily in the chair beside her bed.

"You're not dreaming. I brought you a present, one I've been saving for you, but you'll have to get up to see it."

"Sam, I'm dying, I can barely walk from here to the door. I don't know if I can make it."

He looked at her sharply, a pain flaring in his arm and shoulder, almost taking his breath away. The pain lasted a second, and then faded. "I just sailed over sixty-one hundred miles, by myself, at the age of ninety-five, just to bring you a present. If I can do that, you can get your ass up to see what I brought you."

She looked at him and studied his eyes. The steel in his voice fortified her frail body, giving her a sudden strength. "Alright, you salty old dog, I'll try."

Sam shook his head. "You will and I'll help you."

She moved slowly and to Sara's amazement, she sat up on the side of the bed. With Sam's help she stood, spending most of the energy she'd mustered. She was shaky on her feet, but with Sam on one side and Sara on the other, she made it down the stairs. Jason and Marko helped her into a wheelchair, and then Sam led them outside.

"Your present is tied up at the dock. You just have to go claim it," Sam told her.

She looked at him and started wheeling herself down the path to the dock. Caleb and Kali helped her roll over the planks of the wooden dock until she told them to stop.

"It's her?" Macy said, looking around at Sam. "You kept it all these years?" she asked incredulously.

"I did, she's been with me most of my life. She has survived storms, hurricanes and a six-thousand-mile trip from Rio to North Carolina. Now she's yours, again," he told her while she looked longingly at the sailboat he'd bought her long ago. "The *Emerald* is yours and this time you have to keep it."

She looked at him and her eyes were filled with tears. She turned to Caleb.

"Put me on board," she commanded. "If I'm going to die, I'll die on this boat."

Caleb, Sam and Jason helped her on board and down the stairs to the main salon. Sam led her to the master cabin, holding the door open for her. She sat on the edge of the bed then looked at Sam.

"Stay with me," she pleaded. "I've spent too many years without you by my side. I want to spend what time I have left with you beside me."

"Aye, aye, Captain," he answered.

Sara started to protest but Macy cut her off. "I finally have what I should have spent my whole life with. I'm not leaving this boat or this man until I'm dead. Now go away and leave us alone, or risk seeing us naked," she said in a fiery tone, which booked no argument from her kids.

Sara looked horrified at the comment, looking to Sam for support.

"She's the Captain."

"Damn right I am," Macy affirmed. Sam smiled at the change in her. The salt air seemed to be having a good effect on her.

Sara threw her hands up and left mumbling about how insane the two of them were. Angela and Jason said they would stay with them overnight.

"You don't really want to try and have sex do you?" Sam asked. "We're too old for such foolishness, no matter how much we may want to."

Macy laughed, which turned into a coughing fit. When she stopped she winked at him.

"You're right, but it was fun seeing the look on Sara's face at the suggestion. Besides, it would be a fun way for us to go out."

Sam laughed out loud. "It would, but it would also leave the kids scarred for the rest of their lives."

He joined her on the bed where he held her hand. She clutched him like he would blow away on the breeze.

"I want to go on one last trip," Macy told him.

"Okay, but the kids won't like it," he warned her.

"I'm ninety-five and I haven't sailed in almost thirty years. I want to feel the breeze in my face again and taste the salt spray on my lips. Damn what the kids want, my last wish is one last trip with you."

Sam laughed at her. "Then, as you wish, Captain."

He slept beside her that night and woke up early the next morning to find her sleeping with a smile on her face. He wasn't used to having to share a bed again or sleeping for very long. He joked while cooking supper, he was afraid to sleep too long in case he didn't wake up. Sara and Marko had taken over one of the guest cabins on the boat while Jason and Angela took the other. Caleb and Kali were staying in the house, because there wasn't enough room on the boat for everyone. Sam walked up on deck and checked the weather. It was a beautiful morning and the tide was pulling them away from the dock straining the ropes holding them. Sam cast off the lines and let the tide pull them away. Moving slowly, Macy joined him on deck while he raised the jib and mainsails. She started to sit beside him, but he shook his head.

"You're the captain, you take the wheel."

She sat behind the wheel and he showed her how to tighten and loosen the sails from the cockpit. Sara came storming up from below.

"Are you both crazy? Mother, you're in no condition to go sailing," she shouted at Macy. "And you should know better than to let her do this," she yelled at Sam.

"Sit down and be quiet child," Macy shouted back. "I'm at the end of my life and I don't give a damn about what you think I should or shouldn't be doing. I'm the Captain and I'll do what I want."

Sara pouted, glaring at them. Her shouting brought everyone on deck, to see the house growing smaller behind them. They all begged Macy to turn around, but she refused.

"Sit down, all of you," she shouted over their protests. "I'm your mother and I won't be spoken to like a child. I'm dying and might not see tomorrow, so I'm going to have all the fun I can today. I'm not going to sit in some room and have you wait for me to die. I have my man beside me, the wind in my face and a deck under my feet again. I'll choose my own way for as long as I'm still able. If you keep going on about it, I'll make you to walk the plank."

Sam stood beside her. "She's right, we're almost a hundred years old, we've earned the right to do what we want and not be questioned about it."

Angela and Marko laughed, but Jason and Sara didn't find it funny. Sam's satellite phone rang, interrupting the uneasy silence.

"Where are you?" Caleb asked him. "The boat's gone!"

"We're sailing around the island. Don't worry; we'll be back in a few hours. Your father and your Aunt Sara might have to swim back though."

Caleb laughed over the phone. "Is grandma going to make them walk the plank?"

"She's already threatened it, if they said another word about turning around."

"Have fun, I'll see you when you get back." Sam hung up and looked at Macy wearing a smile. "I knew I raised that boy right."

She laughed, but it turned into another coughing fit. Sara appeared and started to tell her to head back but Macy stopped her with a sharp look.

"I'll return when I am ready, now go fetch me some coffee," she ordered. "And bring some for my First Mate, too."

Sam heard Marko and Angela laughing from below. They returned around lunch time with Marko and Jason racing to tie them to the dock. Sara was still angry and sulked while walking to the house, muttering under her breath. Macy went back to the room to rest while Sam followed.

"Thank you," Macy said, once she lay down. "That was the most fun I've had in a long time. It felt good sailing with you again. If I see tomorrow, we'll have to do it again."

Sam started to reply when he felt a sharp pain in his chest and shoulder. He took a couple of deep breaths and the pain faded somewhat. Beside him Macy had closed her eyes, a peaceful smile on her lips. Sam decided he could probably use a nap, too.

He dreamed again, but this one felt different. In his dream, he saw Shara and Macy standing together on the shore of a beautiful beach where crystal clear waves crashed against the shore. He looked around at the brilliant green grass stretching away from the shore, leading to a city which seemed to glow. A large group of people were walking toward them and Sam could have sworn he saw his parents and many of his friends who had long ago passed away in the crowd. When he looked back at Shara and Macy, they were standing before him smiling.

"It has been too long, my love," Shara said, wrapping her arms around him.

Sam could feel the warmth of her arms and body pressed to his, bringing tears to his eyes while he held her, praying he wouldn't wake up yet.

"Yes, it has," his voice cracking with emotion. "Where are we?"

"Before I answer, there are a few people who have been waiting a lot longer than I have to see you again," she replied, turning him to face the growing crowd. Sam was overwhelmed when he saw his parents and Alex standing there. Behind them were his grandparents from both sides of his family. There was a long period of hugs and kisses while Sam was welcomed into their midst. Somewhere along the way, he figured it out. He turned back and looked at Shara.

"This is Heaven, isn't it?" he asked.

"Still as smart as ever," she said. "Yes, you had a heart attack during your nap and now we're together again."

He looked at her while Macy stood beside Alex. "Macy, too?"

Shara nodded. "Just a few moments before you. We never had a chance to talk until now, but I like her. We have both shared your love on earth and now we will share it here, too."

Jason went to wake his parents for lunch and found them unresponsive. He called for an ambulance, but after EMS arrived the technicians told the family there was nothing they could do. Caleb, Kali and Angela made calls to the few family members they had left on each side to let them know.

Two days later, a man showed up from Brazil and introduced himself to the family. Caleb smiled, recognizing him.

"This was Pop's lawyer from Rio," he explained to his dad. "Pop evidently left a will there."

Kali translated while the man read Sam's will and last wishes. His home in Rio was left to Caleb and Kali. *Emerald* was left to Jason and Sara together to do with what they wished. Kali choked up when she translated the last line in his will.

"My final wish is to be laid to rest with the three women I spent my life in love with. I wish to be cremated and have some of my ashes buried here with Macy, some with my beloved Shara, in Rio and the rest scattered to the wind and sea, who has been my mistress for most of my life," she read slowly. "Love to you all, Sam."

Jason had to change the plans for his father at the last minute. The service in North Carolina was held at the McCoy family cemetery. Jason couldn't help but wonder if his grandfather was furious about Sam being buried in the family plot. The thought actually made him smile a little when they buried Sam's ashes next to Macy. Jason told Michael and Mark about his thought when they got back to the house and they all shared a laugh at the thought of George's reaction.

The ceremony in Rio was just as sad and somber, though many more people showed up to show their support for the family and say farewell. Jason was amazed to see how many people his father had influenced in his time there. Caleb planned a party in his grandfather's honor and everyone in the community showed up to tell stories and dance. The party lasted until the wee hours of the morning because no one wanted to leave.

The most difficult ceremony for all of them was the one to spread Sam's ashes on the sea. For the first time ever, all of the crews, captains and ships of Paradise Shipping and Cruise Lines were assembled to pay their respect. Doug Stephens was the master of the ceremony.

"Sam was a great friend, boss and captain. He and I traveled a lot, drank a lot and made a lot of money doing something we both loved. He was my best friend and he'll be sorely missed," Doug said, his voice trailing off to a weepy whisper.

Caleb took the ashes to the Carolina's bow and released them into the wind while the Quartermaster, Solomon, piped Sam off the ship. The officer of the deck rang the ship's bell once for each decade Sam had served, then piped "end of watch". Caleb joined his wife at the wheel, before addressing the crew.

"Pop had a last request for his crews, he mentioned to me long ago. Everyone who knew him and served with him understood he had a taste for rum." Two stewards rolled out four large casks of Jamaican rum and several trays of glasses.

"He wished for a toast to his crews and one for himself, and that's what we'll do," Caleb said, waiting for a steward to hand everyone a pair of shot glasses.

They waited until everyone had received their two shots before continuing.

"First of all," Caleb said. "To Captain Sam Richards, may his life be an example to us, both professionally and personally. May we find ourselves able to stand worthy in his eyes!" He said lifting one glass to the sky.

Everyone toasted their former captain and tossed back the first shot.

"To what he called the best and most loyal crews in all of the Seven Seas!" he said, holding up the other shot. "May you serve in his memory with honor and pride!"

Everyone tossed back the other shot and cheered.

The party after the memorial lasted the rest of the day. In the Captain's quarters of the *Carolina*, the captains of every ship in the fleet, along with the family, gathered for a private ceremony. Kali poured them all a shot of rum from a smaller cask. Jason stood at the desk and looked around at the men and women present.

"My father loved you all," he said sadly. "Each of you served under his leadership at some point in your careers and you know the kind of man he was. He cared for the people he sailed with, he treated them like family. That's why we feel his loss so deeply. All of you know the story of my father and mother; if their story teaches us anything, it's true love endures, forever. To Sam: Father, Captain, Sailor and Friend."

There were no dry eyes in the cabin when they tossed back the shot. Caleb and Kali stood behind the desk where Sam had spent over half his life. Caleb reached up and wiped his eyes, while Kali clung to his arm, with her head on his shoulder. Beside them, unseen by everyone, Sam, Shara and Macy stood watching the ceremony in silence.

"I'm going to miss the old man," Caleb said sadly.

Doug put his hand on the boy's shoulder. "It wouldn't surprise me if he was here watching all this with a twinkle in his eye. You know, of all the members of his family, you remind me of him the most. He'll never be gone while you're around."

"He's right, sometimes I see you do something or say something and I swear it's Sam moving you like a puppet," Kali told her husband.

Caleb shook his head. "I guess all those years of taking care of him made me more like him than I thought."

"It's not a bad thing, when you take over the business, it'll be like having him back again," Doug explained.

The thought comforted Caleb making him smile. Kali kissed him on the cheek before excusing herself and walking away.

Sam felt a nudge on his arm.

"I told you he was more like you than Jason," Macy said.

"He should be, Lord knows I tried to raise the McCoy out of him," Sam answered.

"I think you did a great job with him. He's a good man, like his grandfather. He deals fairly with people and loves his wife dearly. He's going to be so excited when he finds out about Kali," Shara said with a smile.

Sam moved around to look into his grandson's eyes. He longed to hold the boy again, like he used to when he was a child, and tell him everything would be alright. Also, to tell him the child his wife was carrying would bring all the joy he could ever imagine into his life and make him complete.

Sam felt Shara's gentle touch on his arm.

"We should leave them to their memories," she said softly.

Sam looked at her and nodded. Macy took his hand and slowly the three of them floated to the top of the cabin. Sam looked one last time at the people he loved before passing through the deck and into the sunlight. Drifting up into the rigging, he saw the crews from his fleet dancing and laughing together in the warm Caribbean breeze. Serenity filled him completely while he drifted away…

About the Author

Garry Richardson lives in the small town of Ridgeland, South Carolina with his lovely wife, two amazing kids, their dog Millie and cat Nova. When he's not working, he can be found in his boat throwing a shrimp net, on a baseball field umpiring and occasionally, writing.